Laughter came easily to Piper, Mitch noticed, despite the deep well of dark emotion that he had glimpsed behind that pretty face earlier. A quick smile and an impish sense of humor were second nature to Piper Wynne, but they did not disguise her pain.

She was harboring some sort of secret; yet when her amber eyes lit with that personal sense of the absurd, Mitch couldn't help smiling. Something in her spoke to him.

After dinner she insisted on helping his mother clean up. He could hear the women chatting as he rose to follow his father into the den. He'd have stayed were he was and eavesdropped on the conversation if he could have—not because he particularly wanted to know what they were talking about, but just to hear their voices. Listening to the two of them talking together made him feel peaceful and cozy.

Why had he waited so long to start looking for someone with whom to share his life?

Books by Arlene James

Love Inspired

*The Perfect Wedding #3
*An Old-Fashioned Love #9
*A Wife Worth Waiting For #14
*With Baby in Mind #21
The Heart's Voice #261
To Heal a Heart #285

*Everyday Miracles

ARLENE JAMES

says, "Camp meetings, mission work and the church where my parents and grandparents were prominent members permeate my Oklahoma childhood memories. It was a golden time, which sustains me yet. However, only as a young, widowed mother did I truly begin growing in my personal relationship with the Lord. Through adversity, He blessed me in countless ways, one of which is a second marriage so loving and romantic it still feels like courtship!"

The author of over sixty novels, Arlene James now resides outside of Dallas, Texas, with her husband. Arlene says, "The rewards of motherhood have indeed been extraordinary for me. Yet I've looked forward to this new stage of my life." Her need to write is greater than ever, a fact that frankly amazes her, as she's been at it since the eighth grade!

TO HEAL
A HEART

ARLENE JAMES

Steeple
Hill®

Published by Steeple Hill Books™

STEEPLE HILL BOOKS

Steeple
Hill®

ISBN 0-373-87295-X

TO HEAL A HEART

Copyright © 2005 by Deborah Rather

www.SteepleHill.com

Printed in U.S.A.

Even though I walk through the valley of the shadow of death, I fear no evil; for Thou art with me. Thou dost prepare a table before me in the presence of my enemies; Thou has anointed my head with oil; my cup overflows.

—*Psalms* 23:4–5

Chapter One

The first day of September was shaping up to be one for the record books, Mitch thought wryly, jogging down the airport causeway, briefcase containing his laptop computer in one hand.

First he'd overslept, unaware that the electricity had been off for several hours during the night due to an industrial accident that had taken out a transformer. As a result, he'd missed the early flight to Houston. To make matters worse, in his haste he'd grabbed a pair of mismatched socks and hadn't realized it until he'd looked down while retrieving a dropped pen during a witness deposition. The witness, a prim and proper middle-aged woman, had already been irritated because Mitch had shown up more than an hour late for their appointment. One look at his black-and-blue-sock combination and she'd become convinced that he was a "low-budget shyster," to be exact, and had terminated the interview.

As if that weren't bad enough, he'd been caught in one of Houston's infamous traffic jams and was in danger of missing his return flight to Dallas. Thank God for cell phones and understanding shuttle bus drivers. They'd sped all the way from the rental car agency to the terminal, taking turns without an inch to spare and gunning through a yellow light along the way. The worst part was that he hadn't gotten the information he needed to prevent his client from receiving a stiff sentence for what had essentially been a foolish prank.

Maybe God was trying to tell him something. It wasn't the first time Mitch had thought about slowing down, maybe lightening his case load a little, but work had been his focus for so long now, he wasn't sure what he'd be slowing down for. If he did manage to make the flight, maybe he could find time later that evening to think about some important personal issues, like his priorities and his future.

He rounded a column and jogged into the waiting area of Gate 27 just as the ticket agent was about to close the boarding-ramp door.

"Wait!"

The agent, a stocky Hispanic male, turned, smiled and inquired, "Mr. Sayer?"

Nodding, Mitch came to a stop and bent forward slightly, gasping, "Did I make it?"

"Barely," he answered as Mitch set down his briefcase and batted back the side of his suit coat to fish his ID from the front pocket of his pants. "If you hadn't called ahead, I'd have given away your seat and already released the plane."

"Thanks for waiting," Mitch said, lifting his briefcase from the floor.

The man checked his identification, nodded and stepped back. "Have a nice day."

Mitch smiled and flipped his wallet closed, slipping past the barrier tape to the door beyond, briefcase in hand. He heard the ticket agent radio the flight attendant to reopen the hatch as he trotted down the enclosed ramp.

Just as Mitch rounded a sharp turn, he spotted a folded sheet of paper on the floor. Small and lined, it looked to be filled on both sides with handwriting. Thinking that someone who had boarded the plane before him might have dropped some important notes, he scooped up the paper. The hatch slid open just then, and an attractive brunette female flight attendant smiled at him.

"Find a seat quickly," she instructed as he twisted past her. "We've got an immediate departure window."

Mitch meant to hand her the sheet of paper he'd found, but she hurried away the instant the hatch was secured. Not wanting to hold things up a second longer, Mitch shrugged and slipped the paper into his suit coat pocket as he made his way down the narrow aisle between the seats. Spying an open place about halfway down, he made for it quickly.

The passenger in the aisle seat looked up as he neared. Warm amber eyes regarded him politely. A small but plump mouth curved into a rosy smile. He noted the bright, healthy sheen of light coppery-blond hair smoothed neatly over her head and culminating in a long, thick braid that draped across one shoulder. He forgot all about the sheet of paper in his pocket.

"Excuse me," he said, aware that his voice had deepened. "May I slip in?"

She tilted her pretty head, looking him over quickly. Her high, wide cheekbones, pert nose and slightly pointed chin gave her face a gamine appearance that he found utterly charming.

"It'll be easier if I move over," she said, releasing her safety belt.

She lifted the arm that separated the seats and slid to the center space, next to a gaunt adolescent girl too interested in her fashion magazine to notice much of anything else.

Mitch stuffed his briefcase into an overhead bin and dropped into the aisle seat just as the flight attendant approached to secure the storage locker. He reached for his safety belt as the plane began to creep backward from the bay. Mitch snapped his belt, and the attendant went on her way. Immediately he offered his hand to the pretty strawberry blonde, a little surprised at himself.

"Mitchell Sayer."

She placed her small, cool hand in his. Her nails, he noticed, were short and bare of polish.

"Piper Wynne."

"That's an unusual name," he heard himself saying, "but a lovely one." It also seemed oddly familiar, but he couldn't imagine why.

She laughed and took back her hand, which he realized only then that he'd held too long. "Thank you, and no, I wasn't named after an airplane. It was a bird, actually."

"I'm guessing that would be the sandpiper."

She cocked her head. "Yes. How did you know?"

He folded his arms, not lamenting the close confines for once. "Seemed a logical conclusion."

"You're a birder then, are you?"

"No, not particularly, but I always read the nature magazines we get at the office."

"Office," she mused, tapping her chin with the tip of one forefinger. "And if you're getting magazines by subscription, then you must have people waiting to see you. So what are you? Doctor, dentist…"

"Attorney," he supplied.

"Ah."

"And the magazines are usually for the people who sometimes accompany my clients. I have a thing about keeping people waiting."

"A prompt attorney?" she quizzed with mock skepticism.

He laughed. "Evidence notwithstanding."

She smiled and tugged at the hem of her moss-green straight knit skirt as she crossed her legs. A small woman with small feet and hands, the latter happily devoid of rings, she cut a trim figure in the knit top and tailored jacket that matched her skirt. Mitch looked away, a little embarrassed that he had noticed both her ring finger and her shape, but then he looked back again, too interested to let the connection drop.

"Tell me about this sandpiper association," he said, settling back to listen.

She laughed and began relating her mother's fascination with the quick, darting shorebirds that migrated yearly to the Far East. Again something tugged at his memory, some note of familiarity, but he was quite certain that he had never met the captivating Miss Piper Wynne. She was so captivating that only when the flight attendant returned to offer them a drink did Mitch even realize that they were in the air.

Piper waited several seconds for Mitchell Sayer to give the attendant his drink order, but she realized that he was waiting for her to do the same thing. Only after she had expressed a preference for water and the girl next to her had requested a diet cola did he ask the flight attendant for tomato juice, confiding off-handedly, "My mother's a big believer in vitamin C."

"Maybe you'd prefer orange juice," the flight attendant suggested, but Mitchell shook his head.

"I would like some hot sauce or pepper, though."

The attendant searched the cart for pepper packets even as she poured diet cola into a plastic cup of ice. Seat trays came down, tiny napkins were dispensed and the drinks were passed. Piper noticed that Mitchell didn't so much as open a pepper packet until she and the girl next to her had tasted their drinks.

She smiled over the rim of her cup. He was a real gentleman and a very attractive one. Big and ruggedly handsome, with dark, slightly wavy hair and wide, deep blue eyes, he possessed an air of quiet confidence coupled with a boyish charm that eased into a quick, dimpled smile. Piper took the smile as a sign that her new life was getting off to a promising start.

Instantly her brother's face flashed before her mind's eye. Startled by the doubt that lanced through her, she gulped water and fixed her attention on the man at her side. Having stirred several packets of pepper into his tomato juice with a swizzle stick, he was sipping the bright red brew experimentally.

"How is it?" she asked.

He shrugged and said, "Too salty. I prefer to make my own, and lace it with hot sauce."

"A purist," she pronounced, smiling at him, "with a taste for spicy foods."

He chuckled, his velvet-blue eyes crinkling at the edges. She wondered if he was married. He took another drink, then lifted his arm to check the time on his wristwatch. She noticed that he wore no wedding ring—so, it wouldn't hurt to flirt a little. Would it?

She didn't for an instant think anything would come of this chance encounter, but it seemed an important omen somehow—not that she actually had doubts about this move. She was determined to enjoy every moment life had to offer from here on out. No more crisis management with roller-coaster emotions for her. She was finished with risk assessments and double shifts, second-guessing every move made in the heat of the moment and those soul-tearing life-and-death decisions. Especially the latter.

Exhaustion, guilt and heartbreak had all been left behind in Houston with the emergency-room nursing position that had engendered them. Piper was determined to find relief and happiness in Dallas, beginning now—and who knew? One day she might even meet a special man. Twenty-six certainly wasn't too young to be thinking about marriage and family. Twisting in her seat, she pasted on a bright smile and caught herself literally fluttering her eyelashes.

"I bet your favorite food is Mexican," she said.

"My favorite food is edible," he quipped. Then he admitted, "I do love a good tamale, though…and blackened steak, Indian curry, Italian *diavolo,* Szechuan Chinese, anything spicy. My mother says that if you put enough peppers on old shoes, I'd eat them."

Piper laughed, ignoring an underlying and all-too-familiar pang. Firmly she told herself that all the tears and grief and self-flagellation in the world would not change anything. Why not laugh? After all, she was just trying to follow her father's advice. He was so fond of saying, "God expects His people to face life's difficulties with smiles and cheer rather than tears and recrimination." That's all she was trying to do—find some smiles and cheer with which to face the rest of her life.

She forced herself to think of a clever rejoinder to the handsome attorney's banter, and pretended that the world was a bright and sunny place. The warm smile and pithy remarks of the man beside her coaxed her to think she had made the right decision in pulling up stakes and starting a brand-new life. She couldn't remember the last time she'd enjoyed herself so much.

By the time the airplane touched down at Dallas Love Field, she was congratulating herself on the wisdom of this move. Everything was going to work out fine. It was just a pity that Mitchell Sayer would play such a small part in it all, but she didn't fool herself that his interest was more than momentary. A handsome, successful man like him would never seriously pursue a confused, worn-out ex-nurse. Entertaining conversation was one thing; real life was something else, and that was all she was hoping for—something else. It couldn't be worse than what she'd left behind.

Standing back to let a lady exit in front of him was as natural to Mitchell Sayer as breathing. He didn't think twice about stepping into the aisle and blocking the flow of traffic while Piper and their teenaged seatmate slipped out into the narrow aisle and began making their way forward. The usual rush to deplane was in full swing by that time, of course, so those seated ahead of them naturally took advantage of the short pause to pop up and fall in behind the two females.

Then, of course, the woman seated across the aisle from him must naturally be accorded the same civility as the other women in his immediate vicinity, and before he knew what was happening, half the people on the plane were between him and that bright, quickly receding head.

A momentary sense of loss seized him, but then reason returned, the product of a long-held and carefully nurtured faith. Without even thinking it, without the words forming in his mind, he reminded himself that God was in control of his life. What was truly his would return to him; what was vital to his well-being God would supply. Long ago Mitch had intentionally yielded his life and heart to a loving God. That did not mean, of course, that he didn't hope Piper would be waiting for him when he reached the gate area.

He stepped into the busy airport expectantly, and when he did not immediately spot that shiny pale copper hair, he sidestepped the traffic and took a good look around. Piper Wynne was nowhere to be seen, and he felt a pronounced disappointment.

He had seen his last of that gamine smile and those mysterious amber eyes, behind which he had sensed deep wells of emotion. They had not even said goodbye. Well, at the very least she had given him a wakeup call.

Since the death of his wife, Anne, Mitch had wondered if God meant him to live the rest of his life alone. His parents and his friends all said not, that if ever a man were meant to be a husband and father, it was him. Eventually, and for some time, he had actively dated—a lot. Yet as the years had passed, he'd begun to wonder. His work was important, requiring great dedication and much time, and his personal ministry brought him untold satisfaction and fulfillment. Perhaps that should be enough.

For a long time it had been enough, but lately something had changed. He'd started wondering if he hadn't filled his life with work instead of people. Now he knew of one bright young lady for whom he'd like to find a place in his life.

Just how had that happened?

He'd spent not quite three-quarters of an hour with a sunny, fetching woman, and suddenly the part of his heart that had been dormant was awakened. A need that he had believed dead suddenly lived and breathed inside him. And why not? He was only thirty-eight as of August 11 just past. He was still young enough to find love, marry and start a family, and he realized suddenly that he still wanted to do that, wanted all, in fact, that manhood could afford him—things he hadn't felt able to face in a long time.

A sense of quiet wonder rose inside him. He had trusted God to set the course of his life, and the journey obviously still had some surprising twists and turns ahead. Maybe Miss Piper Wynne was not a part of it, but she was certainly a signpost on the path that he might take, and a very pretty signpost at that. He smiled to himself, adjusted his grip on the handle of his briefcase and set off, content to let God unfold the pathway as He would.

Ten minutes later he slid behind the wheel of his luxury sedan and glanced at the time readout in the dashboard. He still had time to change into jeans before arriving at his parents' house for dinner. As he drove through the city to his University Park home, he thought about how invigorated and hopeful he suddenly felt, as if God had tapped him on the shoulder and whispered a delightful secret in his ear.

He left the car in the drive and let himself into the house through the front door. Walking straight past the seldom-used living room, he went through the open French doors into the study and punched the button on the answering machine on a corner of the cluttered desk. He turned up the volume so he could listen to his messages as he changed clothes in the next room.

As he was unbuttoning his shirt, the rustle of paper in the front pocket of his coat reminded him again of the notes he had found. He hoped they weren't important, because it was too late now to do anything about returning the sheet to its owner. Might as well just toss it. Before he could follow that thought with action, however, the answering machine beeped and the familiar voice of a local assistant district attorney reached his ears. The woman whom Mitch had gone to Houston to interview had called the D.A.'s office. She'd remembered something after he'd left, and while he'd been fighting traffic she'd called the district attorney with the information.

Mitch tossed aside the jacket and rushed back into the study to take notes. He wasn't surprised that she had called the D.A. instead of him. Most witnesses considered the district attorney to be an ally and the defense attorney an unprincipled enemy out to free criminals to pillage and plunder at will. Few realized that all exculpatory evidence must be shared, by law, with the defense. Few stopped to consider who might champion their cause if they should find themselves facing unexpected criminal charges.

By the time Mitch had the details on paper, he was

elated to think that his client, a teenager, would be spared the horrors of prison. Mitch didn't delude himself that the young man was blameless, but the mitigating factors that had come to light had induced the district attorney to offer probation and a fine. Eager to tell the boy's parents, he made a phone call. They were relieved, but still laboring under the disappointment of their son's poor judgment and its results. Mitch figured that the kid would think twice before he pulled another ''prank'' that could end in injury to an innocent third party.

Eager to see his own parents, Mitch hurriedly popped out the tape, locked it in a fireproof file cabinet until it could be formally transcribed and finished changing his clothes. All the while, he kept thinking that God had definitely moved this day in awesome and definite ways.

Marian Sayer pressed her hands together in a typical expression of delight, her elbows braced against the dark wood of the kitchen table, where the family had dined. Though retired from the classroom for several years now, she had never lost her ''teacher'' mannerisms, the slightly exaggerated gestures and articulations that so easily captivated the attention of children.

''Why, that's wonderful, Mitchell!'' she was saying. ''What a lovely ending to a difficult day. I'm happy for your client.''

Vernon nodded sagely. ''Sometimes God lets us think we've blown it just so He can remind us that we're not the ones in charge.''

''Don't I know it,'' Mitch said, grinning again.

"Your cases don't usually put that sparkle in your eye, though," Vernon noted astutely.

Mitch felt his grin grow even wider. His father knew him too well. "Let's just say that I had another 'interview' of sorts today, and it let me know that I'm ready to make some changes in my life."

"How so?" his mother asked expectantly.

He shrugged, trying to keep the conversation casual as he related how he'd met Piper Wynne.

"What did you say her name is?" his mother asked after he'd told as much as he intended to.

"Her name's Piper Wynne," he answered, taking a sip of iced tea so as to savor the taste on his tongue. "But that's not important, Mom. I'll probably never see her again. The point is, I realized today how very much I want to have someone in my life again. I think God's been trying to tell me for some time that it is a possibility."

Vernon Sayer removed the stem of his unlit pipe from his mouth. Typically, removal of the pipe weighted whatever words followed with significance. His father hadn't actually smoked that pipe in years, but he often sucked on it just as if he did. It was part of his dignified lawyer persona, and it had stayed with him even after retirement and the doctor had made him understand how harmful tobacco was to his health. Half a decade later Vernon still hadn't given up the pipe. The tobacco, yes; the pipe, no.

"You're finally ready for a wife and family," Vernon announced.

"Let's just say that I'm ready whenever God is," Mitch clarified, then lifted an eyebrow at the dramatic flourish Vernon employed as he waved the pipe through the air.

"Well, it's about time. Your mother's not getting any younger, you know, and you're her only hope of having a brood of rowdy rug rats scampering around here one of these days."

Mitch laughed outright. His dad was an endless source of dry witticisms and pure delight for him. His mother, on the other hand, was patience and acceptance personified. They were wonderful parents, and they deserved to be grandparents. Perhaps they would be. Surely God was about to bring someone special into his life.

Their joy at the prospect humbled him. For so long he had rejected the very idea of marrying again. He wondered now if he hadn't let his grief over Anne cheat his parents of a grandchild. Though he'd always been keenly aware that, as an only child, he was a major supplier of his parents' happiness, Mitch had never felt pressured to fulfill some parent-defined role of the good son. Goodness, consideration and integrity were expected of him—yes, even presumed—but he had always felt free to be his own person, to live by his own rules and expectations. Now he wondered if he hadn't been selfish—and he'd always thought of himself as such a loving son.

Oh, he had fought the usual adolescent battles, demanding more freedom than he was entitled to or able to handle, but eventually he had come to understand and appreciate what wonderful parents God had given him. They trusted the man he had become. They trusted his faith and abilities, and he trusted their judgment, wisdom and love implicitly, so he pretty much told them everything—had since reaching adulthood. That had helped him in unexpected ways after Anne.

Maybe he didn't call his parents every day anymore, but he did try to get over for dinner once a week, and he never hesitated to pick up the phone and ask for advice if he needed it. For the first time, that didn't seem enough. He owed them more than simple thoughtfulness.

They sat at the kitchen table for a while longer, talking over the day's events. Mitch was as comfortable in this house as in his own home. He'd grown up here, after all. Yet this was his parents' place, a part of him but not his. Oddly, he had never felt the distinction before. It was as if he now stood, quite unexpectedly, at a crossroads in his life, a vantage point from which he could clearly see much that had before been obscure.

When his dad began to yawn, Mitch rose to leave. As usual, his parents got up and the three of them walked through the house together.

"Glad you could come, son," Vernon said, "and I'm glad that everything worked out as it should. Your client's blessed, and I hope he knows it."

"I think he will," Mitch told him. "Before we part company, I intend to make sure that he realizes God's had His hand on him."

"I rather expect he'll live his life a little differently from now on," Marian said.

"No one walks away from the touch of God unchanged," Mitch observed.

"And that includes you," Vernon said, shaking his pipe at him. "I expect the right little gal will come waltzing into your arms any day now."

Mitch chuckled, kissed his mother and hugged his dad. "From your lips to God's ear," he said, pulling away.

He went out the door and down the walk feeling happy and loved. It had been a good day after all. Perhaps knowing what God had in store for you or why life sometimes unfolded the way it did was impossible, but Mitchell had learned, at very dear cost, that God never did anything without the best interests of His children at heart.

Chapter Two

Mitch next remembered the folded sheet of paper on Thursday when he dropped off his suit at the cleaners and performed one last, hurried search of his pockets. He'd learned the hard way that laundering often rendered writing indecipherable. When he came up with the paper again, he thought about tossing it, but a quick glance at the words revealed the phrasing of a personal letter, not just a bunch of meaningless notes. He pocketed the thing again, instinctively protecting the privacy of the writer and the receiver of the letter.

Later, in his office high above the streets of downtown Dallas, he thought about shredding the sheet, but when he removed it from his pocket, he felt compelled to take another look. It was clearly one of several pages, for it began in the middle of a sentence. Mitch noticed for the first time that the ink was tearstained. His heart wrenched as he began to read the eloquent, carefully penned words.

"...of him will surely never subside," he read,

"and will one day be, not a cross to bear, but a cherished joy. His memory will sustain us until that time, and that's why it is so important that we not forget. The pain makes us want, in its depth and rawness, to do just that, but to forget our dear boy would be to rob us of all the delights he brought into our lives.

"Hold on to that, dear heart. Don't let him go, for if you do, you also let me go, and how can I bear that? To lose you as well as him is more, surely, than God can allow, so I beg you, please don't leave. I need you. We all need you. How he would hate it if he thought that his loss would tear this family apart!

"Whatever you do, please know that I love you. I don't blame you in any way. You will always be my treasured…"

The page ended as it had begun, in the middle of a sentence. Mitch turned it over in his hand once more, as if the rest of it might miraculously appear. He stared for a long time at the blotches near the bottom of the page and felt the heartbreak of their loss.

It seemed to be a letter written from one spouse to another, lamenting the loss of their son and desperately trying to prevent the destruction of the union, but he couldn't be sure of that. He couldn't even tell if it had been written by a man or a woman. All he knew was that God had dropped this into his path for a purpose. Why else would he, an experienced grief counselor, have been the one to find it?

A sense of failure swamped him. Mitch smoothed out the letter on his desk blotter and bent his head over it, confessing his error. He should have looked at the paper the moment he was on the plane. Perhaps its owner could have been found then. Perhaps he could have said the right words to send that person home again to a desperate and loving family.

He thought of the pain of losing Anne so unexpectedly, of the anger, even hatred, that he'd felt for the drunk driver who had so unthinkingly snuffed out her life, and he prayed that God would bring these two back together. He prayed for abatement of their pain, for healing, because it was like having a limb ripped off or your heart torn apart when a loved one died. He prayed for the nourishment of new joy and the balm of sweet memories, for the assurance of salvation and the strength of faith. Finally he prayed— for his own peace of mind as well as that of this family in torment—that the recipient of this letter had been returning home and not running away from it.

Perhaps he would never know the facts, but by the time he lifted his head again, he knew that his involvement with the letter wasn't over yet. Either God had a deeper purpose here than making him aware of his failure or he had not yet correctly divined the depth of it. One thing was for certain: the letter would not be destroyed.

Very carefully he folded the piece of paper, and this time slipped it into his shirt pocket. He would carry it there, over his heart, until he understood why it had fallen into his path. He wondered if he should share this with the group that met on Thursday nights and decided, sensitive as he was to the privacy rights of others, that he would seek the advice of his parents first.

Meanwhile, the business of the day was at hand. He heard voices in his secretary's office and realized that his first appointment had arrived. The door opened, and he came to his feet, handshake at the ready, a weight on his heart. Part mystery, part failure, part ministry, part his own painful experience, it was a burden that he would embrace, welcome, bear with—until God Himself removed it.

Piper stepped down off the bus and turned to the right. In just the space of a single week the route had become familiar, and she was beginning to get a handle on her job as a case reviewer at a health insurance company. The amount of paperwork involved staggered the mind, but she preferred staying busy. If life felt a little flat this morning, well, that was only to be expected after her former frenetic pace. Activity in a big-city emergency room had always bordered on panic. She just needed time to adjust.

The apartment she had rented on Gaston Avenue still felt strange, and she couldn't help wondering if she'd made a mistake selling everything before the move. Maybe if she had her old things around her, it would seem more like home. Then again, how could she start a new life if she surrounded herself with the past? No, it was better this way. The strangeness would wear off.

Besides, the new apartment was too small to accommodate all her old junk. She could manage with rented furnishings for a while. By the time she could buy new, she'd have a better idea what style she really wanted, and instead of the hodgepodge collected over her twenty-six years she'd have a well-coordinated home.

Someone jostled her on the busy downtown street. Murmuring a brief apology, Piper looked up to make eye contact, but the woman strode on ahead without so much as acknowledging her. Piper shrugged and let her gaze slide forward again, only to halt at the sight of a familiar face. The man owning it stopped, too, a smile stretching his mouth as pedestrians darted around him. Piper smiled back, searching for a name.

"Mitch…"

"Sayer," he supplied, angling his broad shoulders as he crossed the busy sidewalk. "Hello, Piper. It's great to see you again."

The man from the airplane. She could hardly believe it.

"Don't tell me your office is around here."

"Right there." He gestured toward the black marble front of a nearby high-rise. "What about you? What brings you downtown?"

"The Medical Specialist Insurance Company," she answered, glancing down the street in that direction. "Went to work there the day after I hit town."

His smile widened even further. "That's wonderful! Good for you."

"Thanks." She glanced at the clock mounted atop a pole on the corner, then at her wristwatch, which was running four minutes ahead. Uncertain which was correct, she knew that she had to move along. "Listen, I've got to get to work. Wouldn't do to be late just a week to the day after I started."

"Right. Okay, but could I ask you something real quick? You boarded the airplane ahead of me. Did you see anyone drop a small, folded sheet of paper— just around that little curve in the ramp?"

She considered a moment, but she really hadn't been watching anyone else that day. Shaking her head, she answered him, "No, sorry, I didn't."

He nodded, huffing with disappointment, and slid his hands into the pockets of his pants. "I see. You wouldn't know the names of anyone else on that flight, would you? I'd like to ask around, see if I can return this paper to the one who lost it."

Again Piper shook her head. "I didn't know a soul on that flight and didn't really meet anyone but you."

He smiled again. "Well, at least there's that, huh?"

"Yes." She returned his smile and started off down the street, knowing that she had to get moving again. "I've really got to go."

"Sure." He pivoted on his heel, watching her move away from him. "Maybe we'll bump into one another again sometime," he called after her.

She shrugged, lifting a hand in farewell, turned her gaze resolutely forward and hurried on, thinking how odd it was that the one person in this city whose name she actually knew should work just a couple blocks down the street from her. She didn't quite know whether she should be pleased or worried about that. After all, Mitch Sayer was just a guy she'd met on an airplane. What did she really know about him? He could turn out to be some kind of crazed stalker or something.

God, she thought, *don't let this be some sort of problem. Don't let me…* The prayer died in her mind.

She didn't even know what to ask for, what to worry about. Every concern seemed trivial and useless now, and she'd had a lot of trouble talking to God lately. She wasn't sure what that was about, but she realized that she really ought to be looking for a church soon. Surely that would rectify the situation. It was just a matter of time, then, time and adjustment.

Stifling a sigh, she lifted her chin and lengthened her stride, determined afresh to make this decision work, to build a new life for herself away from the pain of the past. As far as she could see, she really had no other option.

Mitch watched Piper Wynne's compact form making its way down the busy sidewalk. Wearing serviceable pumps, a neat, navy blue skirt and short plaid jacket, she practically marched at double time toward her place of employment. Either she liked the job, was worried about her performance, or really wanted to get away from him. He hoped it wasn't the latter, because he absolutely hoped to see her again, to get to know her a little better.

It had been so long since he'd pursued such a course that he wasn't quite sure how to go about it, but he figured he could probably muddle his way through, given the opportunity. He didn't really expect much to come of it. They might not have anything in common, might not like each other at all if they got better acquainted, but it was time to move forward again in his life. He might as well start with the pretty little strawberry blonde who'd sparked his interest for the first time in a very long while.

He turned, finally, and moved toward his own building, thinking how pleased his parents would be when he told them that he'd seen her again. He'd been too busy to stop by their place lately, but he was going to drop in soon to show them the letter and get their take on it. On the other hand, they might read too much into what had actually been a very brief meeting. Maybe he should just wait and see what happened before he mentioned encountering Piper Wynne on the street.

He couldn't help thinking, though, that it was some

coincidence that in a city of this size they should wind up working right down the street from each other— not that he actually believed in coincidences. To his mind, it was no accident that he'd run into her again, just as it was no accident that he'd come across that letter that day. Accidents and coincidence were for those who didn't know the Lord or trust in His ways.

Mitch wholeheartedly believed that God controlled the events of a life yielded to Him, so if he were meant to get to know Piper Wynne better, the opportunity to do so would come when the time was right. Likewise, if he were meant to find the owner of that letter, God would show him how to do it and why. Meanwhile, he had clients waiting.

He practically skipped into the building, ready to face the day.

Vernon Sayer laid aside the single, creased sheet of notepaper and reached for his pipe, removing it from his mouth in a prelude to speech. First, however, he cleared his throat. The poignancy of the letter had affected him as much as it had his wife.

"They've obviously lost someone dear to them, perhaps a son or even a father."

"It's so sad," Marian added, shaking her head to emphasize the words.

"And you may be right that there is a higher purpose here," Vernon went on, shifting his large, blocky body, "but I don't think you can really blame yourself for not acting sooner, Mitch. What could you have done? Stood up in the middle of the flight and announced you'd found a letter suggesting that someone was running away from grief?" He shook his head sagely. "No, this has to play out another way or not at all."

Mitch sat forward on the comfortable overstuffed couch that matched his father's easy chair and clasped his hands, forearms braced upon his knees. He was well aware of the physical traits that he shared with his father. To Mitch, looking at Vernon was like looking at his own future face. He found comfort in the character that he saw there, the laugh lines that fanned out from the corners of his intelligent eyes and carved deep grooves of his dimples. Even the leathery, beard-coarsened cheeks spoke of masculine strength, a natural counterpart to his mother's feminine softness, both physically and emotionally. With her comfortable roundness, the thick, gray coil of her hair and naturally enthusiastic concern, Marian was the epitome of everyone's favorite teacher.

"What would you suggest?" he asked of them both. "Where is there to go from here?"

"We will certainly pray about it," Marian put in, but Vernon always took the more pragmatic approach.

"Why don't I run this by Craig Adler? He's just been promoted to some sort of vice presidency at the airline. He might have some ideas."

Mitch straightened in surprise. "Is Mr. Adler still working? I thought he retired some time ago."

Vernon chuckled and stuck his pipe into the corner of his mouth, speaking around it. "They'll have to blast old Craig out of his chair and take him straight from there to the morgue." Narrowing his eyes, he added, "Craig doesn't have any reason to want to stay home and take it easy."

Mitch ducked his head smiling at the not-so-subtle hint. Craig Adler's wife had divorced him nearly twenty years ago, and the experience had so soured him on marriage that he'd remained single. Apparently he'd devoted his life to work ever since. The implication, of course, was that Mitch, too, was in danger of making that same mistake. Obviously he was right to keep mum about meeting Piper again, Mitch deduced. No telling what they'd make of that.

Mitch got his sudden smile under control, looked his dad in the eye and said, "Can't hurt to run it by him, and meanwhile I'll follow Mom's advice." Since she was sitting right next to him, he patted her on the knee.

"Your father didn't mean anything by that last remark," she assured him.

"Yes, I did," Vernon instantly refuted. "Mitch works too much. If he's really interested in finding someone to spend his life with, then he's going to have to cut back on his hours. You said it yourself."

"I also said we should keep our opinions to ourselves," she scolded benignly, shaking a finger at him.

He gave her a droll look over the bowl of his pipe. 'You've been married to me long enough to know better than that."

She rolled her eyes, saw that Mitch was trying not to laugh and threw up her hands. "So I have, you meddling old mother hen."

Vernon clamped the pipe stem between his teeth, looked at his son and quipped, "Ah, the joys of married life."

Mitch laughed at them both. His father grinned unrepentantly while Marian folded her arms in a mock huff. "If it makes you feel any better," he heard himself saying, "I saw her again." So much for keeping quiet.

"Her?" Vernon echoed, forehead beetling.

Marian clasped her hands together. "The girl on the plane! The one with the pretty name."

"Piper Wynne," Mitch confirmed. "Turns out she works just down the street from me, but that's all I know about her. And that's all I have to say on the subject."

"For now," Vernon qualified with a flourish of his pipe. "Well, well," he mused, inserting the stem between his lips again.

Well, well, indeed, Mitch thought, looking at his mother's shining eyes. He couldn't help wondering how long they had kept silent, waiting for him to be ready to love again. It was to be expected from his mother, but his father had shown great restraint and respect. Thinking of his garrulous, take-charge father biting his tongue for only God knew how long stunned Mitch.

He cleared his throat and softly asked, "Have I told you two lately how much I love you?"

Vernon removed the pipe from his mouth, smiled and looked down, brushing at imaginary lint on his thigh. Marian's hand closed tenderly over Mitch's forearm.

"It's always good to hear," she said softly.

Mitch sat back and lightened the moment by asking, "What's for dinner?"

His mother hopped up and headed to the kitchen, answering him over her shoulder, "Your favorite, of course—chicken potpie."

Vernon waited until she was out of earshot before confiding, "When I asked, she told me leftovers." He stuck the pipe between his teeth and winked. "Glad you came over."

Mitch just smiled.

* * *

Piper bit off a chunk of sandwich and momentarily turned her face up to the sun, eyes closed. The air felt like silk today, thanks to unusually mild temperatures and a steady breeze that blew the pollution southward. Chewing rapidly, she looked down at the folded newspaper in her lap, her gaze skimming an article on the so-called megachurches in the area. Suddenly a shadow fell across the newsprint. When it failed to move on, she glanced up.

Mitch Sayer stood in front of her, smiling, a hot dog cradled in a waxed wrapper in one hand, his suit coat draped through the crook of his other arm.

She lowered the newspaper to her lap. "Hello again."

"Hello." He lifted his eyebrows as if for permission to snoop. She nodded slightly, and he tilted his head to get a look at what she was reading. "Looking for a church?"

She thought of it more as preparing to look. "Starting to."

"I'd be delighted if you'd try mine."

She made no reply to that beyond a tight smile, but somehow she wasn't surprised to find that he was a practicing Christian.

"May I sit?" He indicated the stone bench that she was occupying.

She pulled her nylon lunch bag a little closer. "Sure."

Mitch tossed his coat over the end of the bench and sat, biting into the hot dog. She saw that he took it covered in chili, cheese and jalapeño peppers.

"You really do like the spicy stuff, don't you?"

He looked over his meal and said, "This one's

mild. I forgo the onions when I have a meeting too soon after lunch.''

She grinned. "Considerate of you."

"Even murderers and thugs can smell," he quipped. Seeing her shock, he apologized. "Sorry. Little jailhouse humor. I forget it's not always appropriate.''

She shook her head. "No, it's all right. You said you were a lawyer. I just didn't think…"

"Criminal law," he supplied, and she nodded.

"I figured corporate something or other."

"I'm a defense attorney," he told her forthrightly. "Dirty job, but someone's got to do it—someone who actually cares about justice, preferably." He bit off a huge chunk of the chili dog.

"And that would be you," she hazarded.

He nodded, chewing, and swallowed. "I do, actually." He waved a hand. "I consider it more of a calling than a profession, which is not to say that I don't find it exciting at times."

"I can imagine." The emergency room had often been an exciting place to work, too, until… She pushed that thought away. "So, do you have any high-profile clients at the moment?"

"A couple," he answered matter-of-factly, shifting on the hard bench. "You heard about a case where a couple of kids took to playing practical jokes on one another and one of them went wrong, put out the eye of an eleven-year-old?"

She shook her head. "No, I live, er, lived in Houston until recently."

"Well," he said, "my client is the kid who rigged his buddy's lunch box with a small explosion. It wasn't a bomb—it was just supposed to make a pop-

ping sound. Unfortunately, his buddy's little brother
took the wrong lunch box to school that morning, and
he happened to be holding a fork in his fist when he
opened it. You can guess what happened.''

"Oh, that's awful.''

"Sure is, and with school violence on everyone's
mind lately, my client found himself looking at an
attempted murder charge. A Houston lady who just
happened to be visiting her granddaughter for lunch
that day saw the whole thing. If she hadn't remembered seeing a name written on the box top in ink
marker, my client would still be looking at an attempted murder charge. Seems he was not exactly a
fan of his buddy's little brother, and the D.A. was
taking a hard line until my witness remembered seeing that. She's the reason I was on that plane, by the
way. How about you?''

"It was the cheapest airfare,'' she told him honestly.

He chuckled. "Yeah. It's bare bones on those daily
shuttle flights, but that's not what I meant. I was wondering what it is exactly that you do for a living.''

"Oh. I thought I told you.''

"You told me that you work for an insurance company,'' he said before taking another bite of his lunch.

She lifted her sandwich and nibbled at it. "That's
right. Case review. You know, that's where a rejected
claim is appealed, so it goes for review, and I either
have to justify the refusal to pay or offer some settle-
ment.'' She wrinkled her nose, thinking how often
she'd complained about some asinine bureaucrat dic-
tating treatment to facilities like the one where she
used to be employed. "Like you said, somebody's got
to do it.''

"Okay. Gotcha. Go on."

"That's about it," she said.

"What about family?"

"Everyone has family," she answered evasively. "Even you, I assume."

He nodded. "My parents live in the White Rock Lake area to the east of here. What about yours?"

"Oh, they're in Houston."

"So that's where you grew up?"

"No, actually, we lived overseas."

"Really? Whereabouts?"

"Thailand."

"Ah, the sandpipers."

"That's right."

"Must've been interesting."

"Well, I'll tell you, it was quite a culture shock when I came to the States in, like, seventh grade to attend boarding school in Tulsa."

He polished off the chili dog and wiped his mouth and fingers with a napkin that he plucked from the folded wrapper, careful not to get anything on his pristine white shirt or dark tie. "So what you're telling me is that your parents stayed in Thailand?"

"For forty-two years."

He cocked his head. "What business was your father in?"

She looked at her sandwich. "They were missionaries."

She felt it the instant he figured it out. It was as if something *popped.*

"Your father is Ransome Wynne."

"You've heard of him," she said mildly, a little disappointed.

"Oh, my goodness. Heard of him? Ransome and

Charlotte Wynne are giants in the mission field. I heard him speak once, a long time ago. His faith just astounded me.''

Piper nodded and tried to smile, but an ache had started in her chest. She fought it desperately. Her companion seemed not to notice.

''Ransome Wynne,'' he murmured. ''Imagine that.''

Piper stuffed her sandwich back into her bag and hastily rose, glancing blindly at her watch. ''Look at the time. I have to get back.'' She turned away, automatically adding over her shoulder, ''Nice to see you again.''

''Wait a minute,'' he insisted. ''You forgot this.'' Pivoting on her heel, she found him right behind her, the folded newspaper in one hand, his suit coat carried once more in the crook of his arm, as if it just naturally gravitated there. He tapped the paper with a forefinger. ''This is it,'' he said.

''What?''

''My church.'' He lifted the paper a little higher so she could read the small ad tucked in among so many others in the church directory section. ''Maybe I'll see you on Sunday.''

She actually recognized the address as being in her neighborhood, but she didn't say so. ''I'm not sure yet about Sunday.''

''You'd be most welcome.''

She met his gaze then, confirming the interest that his tone had seemed to suggest—personal interest. She took the paper from him and tucked it beneath her arm.

''Thank you,'' she said a trifle breathlessly. ''I have to get back.''

"Yeah, me, too." He snagged the collar of his suit coat with the curve of his forefinger, tossing it over his shoulder. She started off again.

"Bye."

"See you," he called after her, and it sounded as if he might have added under his breath, "Soon," but she couldn't be sure, and she didn't look back. She didn't dare. Something about him brought her raw emotions too close to the surface and made her heart beat just a little too fast. That somehow seemed threatening, since she often wondered if her heart had ceased to function entirely.

Chapter Three

Mitchell was astounded. The most interesting, attractive woman he'd met in years was Ransome and Charlotte Wynne's daughter! How amazing was that? The Wynnes were personal heroes of his. He could only shake his head at the thought of it. His parents would be as blown away as he was—if he told them. *When* he told them, he amended mentally, because of course he would tell them. Eventually.

They might jump to all kinds of unwarranted conclusions if he let that particular cat out of the bag too soon, so he had to think carefully about the timing of it. He didn't want to disappoint them, to get them thinking that he'd found the woman God intended for him, only to come to the conclusion later that such was not the case. Better to see how things developed first.

Eager for that, he wondered when he'd see Piper again, and then realized that he'd let her get away without asking for her telephone number or offering his own. Lifting a hand to the back of his neck, he bemoaned his own thoughtlessness, but then he chuckled. He'd see her again if he was supposed to, maybe as soon as Sunday.

He decided that if she showed up at church he'd introduce her to his parents as the daughter of Ransome and Charlotte Wynne. If she didn't, he'd wait to impart this interesting tidbit until after the next development, provided there was another development. Surely there would be. Surely.

Maybe not romantic developments, though. He sensed a skittishness in her, an uncertainty, as if she weren't quite sure if she liked him. Then again, even if she did *like* him, that was no guarantee she'd be attracted to him, let alone fall in love. With so much thinking ahead, he felt a little deflated.

Maybe he'd wait to see if she came to church before talking about her again to his parents.

A car horn blared. Feeling a little disoriented, he glanced around him, then lifted his arm to check his watch. He had time to stroll back to the office, but instead he found himself hurrying, as if he could make the day go faster and Sunday come sooner.

Piper sighed as she punched in the code that allowed her access to her apartment. A feeling of oppression enveloped her; it wasn't even relieved when she reached shelter. Leaden skies threatened to release their burden of rain any moment. Piper refused to think the oppression might be guilt. She was absolutely determined to be finished with guilt. Why should she feel guilty just because she'd decided to attend a church other than Mitchell Sayer's?

Frankly, it hadn't been a very uplifting experience, even though the people there had seemed friendly.

The music had been familiar, and she couldn't quibble with the pastor's sermon or delivery, but she hadn't felt any "connection." So what? she asked herself. At least she could scratch that particular church off her figurative list. Besides, she didn't owe Mitch Sayer anything. As a matter of fact, she didn't owe anyone anything, not anymore. She was a free agent. Completely free. She didn't have to go to church at all if she didn't want to.

Piper trudged past the stairwell leading to the second floor of the small, recently refurbished apartment house and moved into the open courtyard beyond. She'd rented here because she'd been able to view the apartment over the Internet and because she'd imagined that the waterfall at one end of the swimming pool would provide constant, calming background noise. Not today, however. The soft *plinking* sounds were more from the gloomy rainfall than the fountain.

She dashed to her front door, keys in hand, and wrestled with the lock. By the time she got the door open and swept inside, she was thoroughly misted with rain. Closing the door firmly behind her, she put her back to it and let out a deep sigh.

Silence surrounded her, accenting the emptiness she felt. She shrugged out of her sweater, hung it on the doorknob and plopped down on the rented sofa. Recriminations pummeled her. She should have gone to Mitch's church. She should have gone where she knew someone, but she hadn't because he knew who her parents were, and she was so tired of trying to live up to everyone's ideal of who she should be. Being the brave and saintly Wynnes' daughter was more than she could manage just now, perhaps more than she could ever manage again. She wished Mitchell Sayer didn't know, wished she could be just anyone's daughter and sister. She wished it for her parents' and brother's sakes as well as her own.

It was impossible to change who she was, though, so the best she could do was to change her life. That much she could, would manage. She sat up a little straighter, remembering that one of her neighbors had invited her over for dinner this evening to meet her husband.

Melissa Ninever was a few years younger than Piper, maybe twenty-three or -four, and newly married—a tall, slender young woman with an engaging smile and streaky, light brown hair in a short, trendy cut. Melissa had gone out of her way to make Piper's acquaintance. Her husband, Scott, apparently worked a lot of overtime as a shipping scheduler. Melissa herself worked as a clerk at a rental agency just a few miles up the road and seemed to find herself at loose ends quite a lot. She seemed to need a friend as much as Piper did—and she had no idea that Ransome and Charlotte Wynne were revered the world over for their missionary service.

It was Day Thirteen of her new life, and already Piper had made a friend. That was a good beginning—enough for now. The rest would come, surely. Otherwise, why would she have so easily found a job and an apartment via the Internet even before she had set foot in Dallas? They were confirmation, in her mind, that she had made the right decision. For whatever reason, God wanted her out of Houston. Perhaps if she had listened more closely and been more sensitive to His urgings, she and her family could have been spared the pain of these past weeks and months.

Perhaps she would not have made such unforgivable mistakes.

She bowed her head, but confusion swirled through her, blocking any coherent thought that she might have lifted in prayer, so she got up, walked into the small, single bedroom and began changing into casual clothes, pondering how to fill the next few hours. Lunch had to be prepared, of course, and then cleaned up. For the life of her, though, she couldn't think of any other way to fill the time until she was expected at the Ninevers' upstairs apartment.

The afternoon suddenly seemed as bleak as the weather, but she busied herself flipping channels on the rented television and choosing from her meager wardrobe the next week's outfits. She didn't want to show up for work week after week in the same few articles of clothing. Finally she brushed out her thick, wavy hair, slid a bright blue elastic band over her forehead to hold it in place, put on a matching shirt with her jeans and stepped into her loafers.

Melissa had said to come casual, but Piper wanted to make a good impression on her friend's husband, so she added a pair of simple gold hoop earrings and a bangle bracelet, as well as mascara and a touch of pale coral lipstick. Taking along an umbrella this time, she climbed the corner stairs and followed the landing to the Ninevers' door. Melissa greeted her with a bright smile, and Piper allowed herself to be pulled into the colorful apartment strewn with lava lamps, beaded curtains and tie-dyed fabrics straight out of the early 1970s.

Scott Ninever might have been a year or so older than his young wife, but his sideburns, pale shaggy hair and baggy clothes made him seem younger, as did the inch or so in height that Melissa obviously had on him. His friendly, open manner and kooky sense of humor soon put Piper at ease, and she found him every bit as accepting and intelligent as his wife.

Dinner proved to be nothing more than frozen lasagna and prepackaged salad, which they ate sitting cross-legged on the floor around a large, square coffee table in the living area. Modern rock emanated from a wall-sized stereo system. The dining nook was occupied by a desk and an impressive array of computer equipment that looked right at home with the seventies memorabilia and minimalist metal furniture.

An uncomfortable moment came when the dinner lay spread out on the unconventional dining table and the three of them had arranged themselves comfortably around it. From sheer habit, Piper bowed her head in expectation of a blessing. At least a couple seconds ticked by before she realized that her new friends were carrying on with filling plates and pouring drinks. Realizing her assumptions were erroneous, she quickly picked up her napkin and spread it in her lap, keeping her head down until the burn of color in her cheeks cooled somewhat.

If the Ninevers even noticed, they were too polite to let it be known, and she was soon laughing as Scott lip-synced to the music and played air guitar with his fork while somehow managing to eat his dinner. After the meal, Melissa and Scott quickly cleaned up, working as smoothly together as if they'd been doing so for decades, while Piper sat at the counter separating kitchen from dining-cum-office area and admired Melissa's display of hand-painted tin plates. Next they coaxed her into a silly game of dominoes, again to the accompaniment of rock music and Scott's gyrations.

Reluctantly Piper rose to leave just before ten, warmed when first Melissa then Scott kissed her cheek. She was almost out the door when Melissa stopped her, saying, "Hey, why don't you come with us to the arboretum next Sunday?"

"Hey, yeah, bet you haven't been out there yet," Scott added.

"It's really neat," Melissa told her. "Of course, it's prettiest in the spring, but there's still lots to see."

"It's, like, serene, you know," Scott put in, "and they do concerts on the lawn—classical mostly, some folky stuff, too. You really ought to see it."

"Bring a book," Melissa suggested. "We'll just veg out."

"Guaranteed to relieve stress," Scott said enticingly.

Piper smiled. What could it hurt? It wasn't as if anyone would miss her if she didn't attend church somewhere. Besides, it was just one Sunday. She nodded. "I'd like that."

Melissa gave a little hop and clapped her hands together, which made Scott smile.

"Oh, you're going to love it," Melissa promised. "We'll hook up later and fix what time to meet, okay?"

"Sure. Thanks for the invitation, and for a great evening." Piper started toward the stairs, adding, "Next time, my place."

"Right on," Scott called heartily. "Have a good one!"

"You, too."

She went down the steps feeling pleased. She had made two friends. Life was improving already.

"Mr. Adler, you don't know how much I appreciate this," Mitch said, shaking the older man's hand across the gleaming expanse of a very vice-presidential desk.

"Must be some letter you found," Craig Adler said as he dropped into a sumptuous tan leather chair, exposing a large bald spot in the thinning gray hair on top of his head. "Your father says that you wish to retain possession of it until the owner is found." He waved Mitch into one of three matching leather chairs arranged in a slight arc in front of his desk. Mitch folded himself into the nearest one.

"That's correct. I haven't shared the letter with anyone other than my parents, and I don't intend to. It's a privacy issue, you understand."

Adler smiled. "Spoken like a true lawyer, and frankly, the privacy issue is a real concern to us."

Mitch nodded. "I'm aware that you can't just turn over the flight manifest to me."

"I'm glad you understand that."

"And I also realize that you have no vested interest in seeing the letter go back to its original owner," Mitch added.

"You're right. Even if we wanted to, we couldn't reunite every lost item that we find with its owner. Just holding items of value for claim is a real financial burden, so the less the airline has to do with this the better. But I don't see any real reason not to send out a notice informing everyone on the manifest that a personal item of no actual monetary value has been

recovered and is being held for the owner by you.
Provided we can agree on the ground rules.''

Mitch smiled. It was more than he'd dared hope
for, really. "You just tell me how it has to play. We
can even spell it out in writing, if you like.''

"I'll send you a memo when we're done here,"
Adler said, making a note on a legal pad. "And I
have to tell you that I wouldn't do this for just anyone. Even with assurance that nothing in this letter
you've found could be construed as a legal risk for
the airline, I wouldn't normally go against company
practice like this, not even for a personal friend, but
I know your father, and he says this is important.''

"I'm very grateful, sir, and I'd like to add my re-
assurance to Dad's. This won't come back to bite you,
I promise. My sole intent is to return the letter to its
owner. Anything beyond that is strictly up to that individual.''

"Meaning?''

Mitch shifted uncomfortably. He didn't want to
give away too much, but he realized that Adler was
sticking his neck out here. Choosing his words carefully, he said, "Criminal law is not my only area of
expertise. After Anne died, I got involved in a counseling program that has become something of a personal ministry for me. I think this person might benefit from that.''

Craig Adler tapped a finger on the corner of his
desk consideringly before nodding. "All right. Fair
enough. But what happens if the person who contacts
you isn't the owner of the letter?''

"It seems to me permissible to ask if a contact saw
someone else drop a folded sheet of paper on the

loading ramp and, if so, who. I might get at least a description that way."

Adler nodded. "All right."

Mitch shifted forward. "Would it be okay, do you think, if I asked for the names of anyone traveling with the contact so I could perhaps interview them?"

"Hmm, I suppose, but at no time may you represent yourself as connected to the airline per se."

"Absolutely not. And I promise to document every contact."

"I'm sure I don't have to tell you that some folks may refuse to speak to you, and you have to respect that."

"Of course. It goes without saying."

"Then we understand each other."

"Yes, sir, I believe we do."

"Then I'll have my secretary send the notifications out early next week."

"Thank you, sir." Mitch rose, aware that he'd infringed on this busy man's time, and again offered his hand. Adler didn't bother getting up, just leaned forward and briefly clasped Mitch's hand again.

"If you don't mind me saying so," Adler began, sitting back again, "you don't fit my stereotype of a criminal defense attorney."

Mitch smiled thinly. "I can swim with the sharks when it's necessary."

"Your track record tells me that. All the more reason for my surprise. You seem a very compassionate sort."

"Let me ask you a question," Mitch proposed. "If you were in legal trouble, guilt or innocence aside, wouldn't you want a caring, passionate advocate in your corner?"

Adler's mouth crooked up. "Point taken."

"Thank you again, sir, and if I can ever return the favor, I will, God forbid."

Adler chuckled. "Just let me know how it turns out, will you?"

"As best I can," Mitch promised.

Adler inclined his head. "Always the lawyer. Good enough. Tell that lazy old man of yours that I'm still waiting for that golf game he promised me. And be sure to leave your address and phone number with my secretary on your way out."

"Will do," Mitch promised, and went out the door. He dropped a business card with the attractive young secretary at the desk in the outer office, wished her a nice day and pushed through heavy glass doors to the private elevator just outside. As the elegant, cherry-paneled car whisked toward the ground below, he thanked God for making this possible. He had to believe that he would soon be looking into the eyes of someone who might really need him right now.

"I can't believe I let you talk me into this," Piper gasped, bending forward at the hip, her hands on her knees. Straightening, she reached behind her to pull up a toe and loosen her hamstring.

"I can't believe you kept up so well," Melissa said between gulps of air.

"Oh, please." Piper brought her hands to her hips, feeling the springy fabric of workout tights beneath her fingertips. "You were running slower than usual."

Melissa shook her head. "No way. Well, maybe at first, but only at first."

Pleased, Piper lifted an arm over her head and bent

sideways from the waist, stretching tight muscles. "I am going to be so sore tomorrow!"

"Just stretch out again before you go to bed tonight," Melissa advised, bending and grabbing her ankles. "A little time in the pool wouldn't hurt, either."

"Before or after dinner?"

"Before. I'll have Scott grill us some burgers while we loll."

"Only if I can bring the buns and fixings."

"Deal."

Piper linked her hands behind her and lifted them as high as she could. Melissa straightened and eyed her enviously. "Honestly, I'd kill for that figure."

Piper dropped her arms and looked down at herself. "This figure is why I let you browbeat me into getting up at the crack of dawn to pound the pavement."

"It's about health, not looks," Melissa reminded her. "Not that there's a vain bone in your body."

"Or yours," Piper returned. "Besides, why would you want to be anything other than what you are when Scott thinks you're perfect?"

Melissa grinned. "Why do you think I married him? Hey, how come you're not with anyone?"

Piper shrugged. "I never really had the time to meet guys before, and now I wouldn't have the slightest idea where to look, frankly."

Melissa cut her a sideways glance and mopped her face with the tail of her T-shirt. "Then what would you think about meeting a friend of Scott's?"

Piper instantly pictured a goateed, beatnik type. "Oh, I don't know."

"Actually," Melissa went on, "Nate is Scott's boss. He's almost thirty, real outgoing, kind of a conservative dresser, never been married, makes good money, not bad looking, either, if you like them big and beefy.''

For some reason the picture in Piper's mind dissolved and reformed into the image of Mitchell Sayer. Now, where had that come from? She shook her head. Melissa took it for refusal.

''Aw, come on. What've you got to lose?''

''I'll think about it,'' Piper promised, heading for her apartment door. ''See you later. Provided I can still move.''

''Burgers right here by the pool,'' Melissa reminded her. ''And he really is a good guy!''

''I said I'll think about it.'' Piper tossed the words over her shoulder. But what was there to think about really?

Melissa and Scott were her only friends. Oh, she'd eaten lunch with some of the women at work this week, but no one seemed inclined to socialize outside the office. She enjoyed the time she spent with the Ninevers. The arboretum had proven very enjoyable indeed. Surely she could trust their judgment when it came to this Nate fellow, and she really did want to meet someone special, even though she seldom let herself think about it. She cringed at the thought of a blind date, but she really ought to be more open to the possibilities. After all, what was the point in starting a new life if she kept holding on to the same old attitudes?

She knew that she was going to agree before she even finished her shower and got dressed for work, but she couldn't shake the feeling of trepidation. All day long she kept trying to find excuses for refusing to meet Scott's friend. In the end, however, she couldn't make herself be that dishonest. No good reason existed for not meeting this Nate. She decided to tell Scott at dinner that she would be pleased to meet his friend.

After the bus let her off in front of the apartment house, she hobbled straight to the mailbox in the common area and unlocked her cubby, as was her custom. Most of what she received consisted of circulars and advertisements, but when she came across a letter from the airline upon which she'd flown from Houston, she decided to check it out, although it was probably just a credit card offer or some such thing. Carefully inserting a fingernail beneath the flap, she tore open the envelope and unfolded the single page within.

To her surprise it wasn't some advertising gimmick. Instead it was a note from the office of the vice president saying that a personal article of no real monetary value had been recovered by a third party interested only in returning it to its owner. Anyone having lost such a personal item was instructed to call a local telephone number or write to a local post office box. Piper shook her head. She hadn't lost anything that she knew of—at least nothing that could be returned to her. She dropped the letter into the trash can along with the other junk and headed for her apartment as swiftly as her sore, tight muscles would allow.

By Tuesday of the following week, Mitch had received three replies to the airline mailing—two phone calls from Dallas-area residents and a letter from Houston. The letter writer claimed to have lost a valuable family heirloom in the form of a large diamond ring, despite the airline's specific wording of the notice. Mitch shot off a letter stating, once again, that the item recovered was of no monetary value and definitely not a ring. He suggested that the writer submit a properly documented claim to the airline, while privately doubting that the ring had ever existed.

The telephone calls were no more helpful. One call came from a nervous newlywed whose private honeymoon video had probably never made it on the airplane in the first place. The other came from a wary older gentleman who wouldn't say what he'd lost or give Mitch his full name or address, so Mitch suggested that they meet in a public place.

The man chose a popular Greenville Avenue restaurant, and they set a time for early Friday evening. Mitch felt cautiously optimistic, but it turned out that the fellow had lost his Social Security card and didn't want his daughter to know.

"She thinks I'm the next thing to senile as it is," the grandfatherly man explained.

Mitch advised him to contact the local police and the Social Security Administration immediately, as well as all three national credit reporting agencies and the administrator of his pension checks.

"It's a hassle, but it's the only way to protect yourself, identity theft being such a problem these days. And if you find out someone's been using your information to make purchases or apply for credit cards, let me know right away. I'll go with you to file a report and help you clear your name and credit."

He gave the man his business card, brushed aside his expressions of gratitude and asked if he had seen anyone drop a piece of paper while boarding the plane. Like the newlywed, the gentleman answered in the negative, but he suggested that Mitch ask a friend who had accompanied him on the flight. Mitch jotted down the name and telephone number that was supplied, then insisted on buying the fellow a glass of iced tea and an appetizer. He politely refused Mitch's offer of dinner, so Mitch dined alone, disappointed that he was no closer to finding the owner of the letter, though it was early days yet.

Chapter Four

The restaurant had filled up by the time Mitch was ready to leave—not at all surprising, since the lower Greenville area was a popular nightspot on the weekends. However, Mitch had hardly noticed as he'd sat brooding over his dinner. Only when he looked up to signal the waiter for his check did Mitch realize that the place was alive with movement and conversation. He glanced around him in some surprise, and his gaze snagged on a head as bright as a shiny new copper penny.

She wore her hair down and loose, the sides tucked behind her ears, rather than braided as before, and had applied just a touch of makeup, darkening her lashes and adding sheen to her full lips, but there was no mistaking that face with its wide, almond-shaped eyes, pert nose and slightly pointed chin. She was sitting with three other people, a couple holding hands on top of the table and a man, obviously her date. Mitch felt his stomach muscles clench.

After she hadn't shown up at church that Sunday,

he'd thought about looking her up at work, but he'd told himself he would see her again when he was meant to and that he should concentrate on returning the letter. He had looked for her a couple times in the square where they'd bumped into each other before, but she was evidently taking her lunch elsewhere these days. And now she was seeing someone else. He gulped and passed a hand over his eyes, surprised by the depth of his disappointment.

God knew that she didn't owe him anything or he her, but he couldn't shake the sudden feeling that it was supposed to be different. When the waiter returned with his credit card and receipt, Mitch added a generous tip to the total, signed his name and slipped the card back into his wallet. Rising, he pocketed the whole and prepared to take the long way around the room to the door, but just as he pushed his chair up under the table, Piper turned her head and looked straight at him.

Her amber eyes lit with recognition, and then a small, helpless smile touched her lips. Mitch straightened his tie and began making his way toward her before he even realized that he was going to do so.

Piper glanced at the man beside her. Talking loudly to Scott about some soccer game, he failed to notice either her or the big man approaching them. Nate Tatum was loads of fun, all right—the loud, abrasive type who yammered constantly. He hadn't shut up all evening, going on and on about one thing or another. It wasn't that he ignored her so much as that she wasn't pushy enough to interject herself into his monologue. Melissa kept looking at her apologetically, while Scott worked not to notice how self-involved and boorish his friend was outside the office. Nate was Scott's boss, so what else could Scott do?

Piper sighed inwardly, then admonished herself to lighten up. So Nate was not the man of her dreams— so much not that she never intended to see him again—but she could still enjoy herself. She and Melissa had put their heads together earlier and giggled about a pair of elaborately coiffed standard poodles being walked by a couple in matching sweaters. Later she'd watched one of the few children in the place smear melted cheese in his hair while his oblivious parents perused the menu at length, and now here came Mitch Sayer.

Her heart sped up a bit. Telling herself that she had no reason to be either embarrassed or pleased, she smiled up at him as he drew near.

"Piper."

"Hello, Mitch. Fancy meeting you here."

"Enjoying your dinner, I hope. Mine was excellent."

"We do manage to run into each other with surprising regularity, don't we?"

His dark blue eyes danced with an invitation to share secrets, and she felt her smile widen.

Melissa shifted inquisitively, reminding Piper to make introductions. She literally waved a hand in front of Nate's face to get his attention.

"These are my friends and neighbors, Melissa and Scott Ninever, and their friend, Nate Tatum." *Their* friend. Had she really said "their friend"? Nate didn't even seem to notice. "Guys, this is Mitchell Sayer, the very first person I met in Dallas."

"Technically, it was even before that," he pointed out with a grin.

"Right. On the way to Dallas, I should say."

Mitch nodded at Melissa and shook hands with Scott and Nate, who momentarily dammed the flow of his speech in order to acknowledge the newcomer. Mitch turned his smile right back to Piper.

"So how have you been?"

"Fine, thanks." She glanced at Melissa and coyly added, "Fine but sore, since Melissa here has me hauling myself out at the crack of dawn every morning for laps around the block."

Mitch split a look between them. "Neither of you looks like you deserve that kind of punishment. Now me, if I don't get in at least three miles a day, I start looking like something that came in with the circus, something with a trunk."

Piper laughed, but it was Scott who said, "Hey, man, you must do some weight training, too."

Mitch nodded. "About three times a week, schedule permitting."

"Weights, now that's my deal," Nate announced. "Back in high school I could bench…"

Piper automatically tuned him out. Mitch listened politely for a moment, then he placed one big hand on the edge of the table and the other on the back of her chair as he bent forward, dipping slightly to bring his face close to hers.

"Haven't seen you around lately," he said softly, and her heart skipped a beat at the notion that he had actually been looking for her. She reminded herself that the genie was already out of the bottle where he was concerned.

"As I learn the ropes, they're putting more on me at work," she said. It was the absolute truth—and had nothing whatsoever to do with why she'd avoided returning to the downtown park. She hadn't wanted to run into him, wouldn't allow herself to be pulled back into the trap of other people's expectations of Ransome and Charlotte Wynne's daughter.

"I hope I'll see you again sometime," Mitch told her, holding her gaze with his.

She replied dryly, "Given our track record, it seems likely."

Mitch smiled at that. Then Scott burst out laughing at something Nate said, and Mitch straightened. He nodded around the table, smiled at Piper and said, "Enjoy your evening."

"Thanks. You, too," Piper said as he moved away.

She watched him make for the door and exit onto the sidewalk, alone. Interesting. When she turned back to the table, Nate was chattering on about some new subject. Scott's expression of interest was beginning to look a little strained; Melissa's, however, was rapt, but not for Nate. She lifted both eyebrows at Piper.

Leaning forward, Piper said into her ear, "Just someone I met on the plane from Houston."

Melissa pursed her mouth speculatively, and Piper knew they were going to discuss Mitch Sayer in detail at the first opportunity. To her surprise, she was looking forward to it.

Had he been a betting man, Mitch would have bet his bottom dollar that Piper would be in the park on Monday. He'd have been wrong. She wasn't there on Monday or Tuesday or the day after that. On Thursday it rained—the kind of chill, gloomy rain that warned that winter was truly on its way. When Friday dawned bright with the warm, sweet sunshine that was Texas at its best, Mitch knew he had to get outdoors before it was too late. The rest of the city seemed to feel the same way—everyone but Piper Wynne.

He had a long talk with God about that. If she were part of God's plan for him, then Mitch wished heartily that it be made plain. If not, then he was in need of acceptance and maybe a little patience, not to mention the wisdom to recognize the woman God did have in store for him when she finally came along. Later he remembered one of his father's favorite sayings: Acquiring patience requires patience. Everyone had it, Vernon liked to note, but none liked to exercise it. Mitch discovered that he was no exception.

In the end, what salvaged the week for him were the replies that he got from the airline mailing. He made or received at least one phone call every day, but with no positive results other than a couple leads to follow—names of other passengers given him by the respondents. At least, he told himself, he was doing something positive. The rest was in God's hands.

On Sunday after church, when his parents suggested he accompany them to one of the remaining concerts of the season at the arboretum, he readily agreed. He preferred a concert to a day indoors in front of the television set.

Piper let the bell-like tones of the harp flow over her and turned a page of the paperback novel she was reading. One elbow was braced comfortably upon the back of the bench where she sat beneath an enormous magnolia tree. White Rock Lake shimmered at the foot of the grassy slope before her, reflecting the clear, breathtaking blue of the sky. To her left stood the Spanish Colonial DeGolyer mansion, a structure of gleaming white stucco and red slate that was now park property. Air as soft as silk brushed her skin, and golden sunlight playfully dappled the ground at her feet, sieved through the big waxy leaves whispering softly overhead.

It was a perfect day, the sort that they must have enjoyed in the garden of Eden, exactly the kind of Sunday made for resting from the rigors of a busy week, and it suited her needs perfectly. Since her first visit here with the Ninevers, Piper had made the arboretum her Sunday sanctuary. It was here that she most felt able to commune with God lately.

Someone sat down on the bench next to her, rather closer than she found comfortable. Determined not to allow her peace to be disturbed, she shifted forward slightly, not enough to be rude but enough to create a boundary of sorts. A throat cleared. She ignored it. The next instant her book was plucked neatly from her hands. Aghast, she turned her head sharply to the side—and encountered the smiling face of Mitchell Sayer.

For one second she dangled between outrage and an unexpected pleasure so piercing that it caught her completely off guard. The next moment she was laughing.

"Hello. Again," he said, handing the book back to her.

She earmarked the page and closed it. "Hello yourself."

"I've been wanting to see you," he said baldly.

Some unidentifiable emotion shimmered through her, making her look away. "Have you?"

"Umm-hmm, very much. I keep hoping that you'll take me up on my invitation."

That got her to turn back again. "Invitation?"

"To visit my church."

"Oh." She shrugged and gazed off across the lake to hide the fact that she was flustered. "Right now this is my church. I've found God again in this place."

He cocked his head at that. "Again?"

She blinked. Had she said that?

After a moment he waved a hand in a gesture that included their surroundings. "It's true," he agreed. "God is here." He fixed his gaze on her face, adding softly, "God is everywhere and always available."

Piper shifted uneasily. The conversation was about to wander into areas that she'd rather not visit. She put on a bright smile and changed the subject.

"Are you here for the concert?"

He balanced one ankle atop the opposite knee. "Yes, as a matter of fact, I am. My mother has a true love of the harp. I think she harbored a secret dream that she might raise a harpist, but all she got was me and these." He held out his big, thick hands, smiling. "I always found them more suited to the bass fiddle than the harp."

"Do you actually play the bass fiddle?"

"I do. On occasion. Not particularly well, I'm afraid. What about you? Play any musical instruments?"

Piper wrinkled her nose. "I played flute in high school, but I didn't stick with it."

"Ever thought of taking it up again?"

She shook her head. "No, not really."

"Maybe you should."

"Maybe I will."

A smile stretched his mouth wide, and the effect was just mesmerizing, especially when his gaze touched her lips and lingered there for a moment. She forgot how to breathe until he looked away again and said something about flutes being made for chamber music and the bass fiddle for jazz.

"At least the way I play it," he qualified. "Do you like jazz?"

She shrugged, searching for an answer that should have been right on the tip of her tongue. "Uh."

"It's an acquired taste," he went on easily, "but I find most things are, don't you? Like jalapeños."

"Or coffee."

"Exactly, but really, is there anything better than a good cup of coffee? Especially on a day like this one."

She laughed, feeling that she'd gotten her feet under her again. "When you do what I do, you want the stuff intravenously," she said, then, seeing his look of confusion, she realized what she'd said. *Do.* Not *did.* Before he questioned her, she hurried on. "Now, for pure pleasure I really enjoy a cup of hot tea."

"You and my mother," he said, rolling his eyes. "That's one taste I haven't acquired."

"You should try it sometime."

"Oh, I've tried it plenty," he confessed, leaning sideways slightly. "Mom thinks I love the stuff."

Piper lifted an eyebrow. "Thinks?"

"It's a special thing for her, you know? Once in a while we sit down together over a cup of tea, just the two of us."

"You must love her a great deal," Piper said softly, feeling it like a knife in her heart.

He smiled, nodding. "My folks are really great."

Piper gulped and said, "Mine, too." Suddenly she wanted to cry. Her parents *were* great. *She* was the disappointment, the failure. She swallowed the tears and stared at the lake, blinking. Mitchell's arm slid around her, his hand cupping the knob of her shoulder heavily.

"You must miss them."

She didn't. How could she when she couldn't bear to face them? She pulled in a deep breath, letting him think what he would and forcing the dark feelings back below the surface.

"So where do you play this jazz that you've acquired a taste for?"

Once more he accepted the change of subject with equanimity, his hand falling away from her shoulder. "Here and there. Mostly in the coffeehouse in the basement of our church."

She laughed. "Two acquired tastes in one. Next it'll be goatees, long sideburns and black turtlenecks."

"Oh, yeah, that'd go over big in court."

They both laughed, and talk turned to the courtroom.

He told her about showing up in the same tie as the prosecutor one day, only to have the judge open his robe and display the exact same neckwear.

"Scared my client to death," he said. "He thought we were all in some sort of secret society together and the fix was in." He shook his head. "People in crisis get the strangest notions."

"What happened to his case?"

"Probation and counseling. I hear he enrolled in college this semester."

"That must make you feel good."

"It does."

"What happened to that other kid you told me about? The one who played the prank."

"He got five years probation, a six-thousand-dollar fine and will finish high school at an alternative site. No prom, no sports, no extracurricular activities other than those relating to his counseling."

"Seems harsh."

"Not nearly as harsh as prison."

Before she could respond to that, an older couple approached, arm in arm, and Mitch waved to them. Piper knew at once that they were his parents. For one thing, Mitch greatly resembled his father. Except for the eyes. As the older couple drew near, Piper saw that Mitch definitely had his mother's blue-velvet eyes. He rose, ushering Piper up with him, one hand cupping her elbow.

"Mom, Dad, I want you to meet someone."

Piper detected a very keen interest in both of the elder Sayers. Mitch's hand hovered near the small of Piper's back.

"This is Piper Wynne."

Mrs. Sayer literally clapped her hands together as she inclined her head in greeting.

"What a lovely surprise!"

Piper noticed that she wore her thick, steel-gray hair in a braided coil at the nape of her neck.

After trading a look with his son, Mr. Sayer plucked his cold pipe from his mouth and dropped it unceremoniously into the pocket of his cardigan. He was the tweed-coat type, very professorial looking, right down to the reading glasses perched on the end of his nose. Behind them his eyes sparkled with mischief, belying their muddy-green color, somewhere between light brown and the shade of dried moss. His hair, still thick but receding slightly at the temples, was equal parts brown and silver, as if his head had been dusted with sugar, enough to cloud the rich chocolate color and leave sparkly bits to catch the light. He was a little heavier than Mitch, but toned and healthy looking, whereas his wife was all grandmotherly softness. He offered Piper a handshake. His hand was as broad and flat as Mitch's but more rugged, stiffer.

"Well, Piper, it's a pleasure to meet you."

"Thank you, sir."

"Oh, no, we're Marian and Vernon," Mrs. Sayer—Marian—said, blatantly looking Piper over. "My, my," she commented to Mitch, "you never said how pretty she is."

Piper tossed him a surprised glance, and he had the grace to color slightly, bow his head and cough behind his fist.

"Now, we must get to know one another," Marian instructed, taking Piper's hand in hers.

Mr. Sayer—Vernon—grimaced. "I thought you were going to feed me."

Marian rolled her eyes. "We ate lunch not three hours ago!" She added in an aside to Piper, "You can tell I starve the poor wretch."

Piper bit her lip to hide her smile and felt rather than heard Mitch's chuckle.

Vernon patted his abdomen affectionately. "It's all this fresh air—makes a man peckish."

Marian gave in with a slump of her shoulders. "Oh,

all right.'' She still had Piper's hand in hers, and now she gave it a little tug. ''You'll join us, of course. We can talk more comfortably at the house, anyway.''

Piper blinked. ''Oh, uh.''

Marian looked to her son. ''Mitch, get her to come.'' She gave Piper's hand a squeeze, patted her cheek and busily turned away. ''We'll bring the car around.'' Taking her husband by the arm, she forcibly turned him and headed, ostensibly, toward the front gate. Vernon sent a look over Marian's head to Mitch, winked at Piper and fished his pipe from his pocket as Marian led him away.

Mitch shuffled his feet but said nothing, just waited for Piper to make up her mind whether or not she would accept his mother's insistent, unexpected invitation. Piper frowned, unsure. One part of her wanted to walk away, fast; another recoiled from the swift, painful knowledge that she was more of a coward—and more lonely—than she wanted to admit. Yet somehow all she could think to say was, ''You didn't tell them about my parents.''

He shrugged, but made no explanation. After a moment he said, ''You don't have to come. You could have another engagement.''

She didn't, but she could say that she did. Except that she was not a liar. She wasn't a coward, either, unless she let herself be. She pressed her shoulders back even as confusion surged through her.

He had mentioned her to his parents, but he hadn't mentioned her parents to them for some reason. That seemed significant. It seemed significant enough to tilt the scales in favor of accepting an invitation to dinner. She picked up her book and stuffed it into her small backpack before slinging the pack over her shoulder.

Then she turned and began ambling toward the gate, some distance away.

Mitch fell into step beside her, and she asked him just what he had told his parents about her. He bowed his head, his words as measured as his footsteps.

"That I've met someone I'm interested in."

She let that settle into her thoughts, let it germinate for a few moments and produce a surprising conclusion. She was interested in him, too.

Intellectually she knew that the whole thing was fraught with risk, but as they slowly wandered toward the gate and his parents, she felt an odd comfort in his presence, as well as a growing swell of excitement.

"Is your car here?" he asked after some time.

She shook her head. "Don't have one. I've been getting around by bus."

"That can't be fun in Dallas."

"It's not too bad. The worst is grocery shopping. There's not much close to where I live."

"And that is where?"

"On Gaston Avenue, a few blocks off Abrams."

"I'll see you home whenever you're ready to go."

"You don't have to do that."

"Oh, I'd like to. Besides, it's not far."

She smiled. "All right."

As they drew near the brick columns of the gate, Mitch once more reached out and rested his hand in the small of her back, his touch light, warm, gentlemanly. A full-sized domestic luxury sedan waited at the curb outside, the engine rumbling. Mitch leaned down and opened the rear door. Piper bent forward and ducked inside, her braid swinging down over her shoulder in front. She saw Marian Sayer touch a hand to her own braided coil. Then Mitch dropped down lightly beside Piper, his arm sliding along the back of the seat.

"Wasn't the music lovely?" Marian said, obviously feeling that it was her duty to offer a suitable topic for discussion. Piper smiled, remembering her conversation about music with Mitch earlier.

"Yes. Lovely."

"Do you by chance like jazz, dear?" Marian asked innocently.

Piper sliced a conspiratorial look at Mitch. "I'm told that it's an acquired taste, ma'am."

His mouth quirked, and he gave his head a patient little shake. His mama was matchmaking, and he knew it; he acknowledged it but didn't mind. She found that interesting. The whole Sayer familial relationship was interesting. A man of Mitch's age, confidence and personality did not usually evince such a close, almost indulgent, relationship with his parents. Somehow, rather than making him seem dependent, it made him seem unusually strong.

"Actually," Piper said with sudden conviction, "I do like jazz."

His expression didn't change, but his arm slipped down until it casually rested across the tops of her shoulders.

Perhaps, she thought, she liked jazz even more than she'd realized.

Chapter Five

The drive was short, as the Sayers lived in the White Rock Lake area, but along the way Piper learned that Vernon was a retired attorney, Marian a retired elementary school teacher and Mitch an only child.

"We wanted more," Marian admitted baldly, turning a fond look over her shoulder, "but instead of more children we got the very best."

Mitch chuckled and shook his head.

"Well, we did," she insisted.

Mitch telegraphed a message to Piper. *Mothers.*

Piper telegraphed one back. *She means every word of it.*

He nodded, that small, defenseless smile in place. Piper found herself wondering why he wasn't already attached romantically. As close as he seemed to be to his parents, she sensed that he was very much his own man. Some other woman must have seen what she did. The conviction was growing in Piper that she might have stumbled onto something special.

Vernon pulled the car into the spotless garage of a

long, low, white brick house nestled artfully in the center of a tree-shaded lot. Piper knew instinctively that this was where Mitch had grown up. He let himself out of the car and reached down to assist her. Marian was already on her way to the door before Vernon had killed the engine, making him the last one to get out. Mitch waited for his father to move toward the door before he touched her back as a signal to follow. It seemed a supremely respectful thing to do.

"Come on in, Piper," Vernon said around the pipe stem between his teeth, "and make yourself at home. Son, show her where to go, would you? I'm going to help Mother in the kitchen."

"Of course. This way."

They followed Vernon into a cool hallway floored with white ceramic tile. Piper received the instant impression of comfort and security. She saw gleaming woods, pale walls and good, serviceable furnishings, as well as a smattering of artwork. In the den she found the photos.

Framed and arrayed across one wall as well as on the mantel and tabletops, photos displayed the Sayers as a young couple and Mitch from infancy to adulthood. The most recent, a photo of Mitch receiving an award and shaking hands with another man, couldn't have been more than a few months old, but the one that caught and held her attention was a wedding photo: Mitch in a white tuxedo standing next to a sweet-faced brunette in yards of satin. The photo was at least a decade old.

"Her name was Anne," he said quietly, standing at Piper's elbow, and she knew then why he was not—rather, no longer—attached.

"How did you lose her?"

"Lose her," he echoed, looking down at his toes. "I didn't." He lifted his gaze then, rich blue eyes piercing, open. "She died over nine years ago, but she has never been lost."

Piper gulped and moved away, crossing her arms over her middle protectively. She didn't want to feel what she was suddenly feeling, didn't want to think the thoughts hovering at the edges of her mind. Mitch shifted his stance but didn't come after her. Instead he reached out to her with words.

"Her death has given me a rather unique perspective," he said, "a calling of sorts. I'm a certified grief counselor. We have a group that meets at church."

Piper turned her back on him, desperately clinging to her composure. He went on.

"What I've learned has helped me deal more effectively with my clients and the families of my clients—and sometimes their victims."

Anger flared inside her, along with the irrational notion that she'd been set up for this. She turned on him, speaking more sharply than she intended. "And just what, may I ask, is your 'fix' for grief?"

He stared at her, his head slowly tilting to one side. "Time," he said.

She scoffed at that. "More like a *good* time. Or don't you think that we should enjoy life while we have the chance?"

"All right," he said after a moment, whatever that meant.

She whirled away again, muttering, "A good time just might be all the joy some will ever know."

She felt him move, sensed it in the instant before his big, strong hand closed on her elbow. She turned to face him, but then Vernon was there with a tray of crackers and cheese spiked with olives on toothpicks.

"Appetizers!" he announced jovially. "Mother's putting on the dog."

For an instant Mitch's gaze searched Piper's face, but then he smiled at his father and turned her gently but resolutely toward the sofa, asking, "What can I get you to drink? There are sodas in the fridge under the bar."

"Anything at all," Piper answered stiffly, sinking onto the comfortable sofa.

A moment later Vernon had fixed on a photograph of Mitch in a football uniform and a tale about the day he had finished a game with a broken foot. Gradually Piper felt the ugly tension inside her ease. After a while, she no longer felt as if she might fly apart at any unguarded moment, and her enjoyment in her company and surroundings returned.

Laughter came easily to her, Mitch noticed, despite the deep well of dark emotion that he had glimpsed behind that pretty face earlier. A quick smile and an impish sense of humor were second nature to Piper Wynne, but they did not disguise her pain. His trained eye recognized the signs. She was harboring some sort of secret, some serious, perhaps overwhelming problem; yet when those amber eyes of hers lit with that personal sense of the absurd, Mitch couldn't help smiling, even when he didn't know what had struck her as funny.

His parents were a little befuddled by her. They were hopeful, almost pathetically so, although she was nothing like quiet, reserved, delicate Anne. He wondered what it was about her that made his nerve endings tingle with awareness. It was more than her pretty face and womanly figure. Something in her spoke to him. It was as if he knew her on some very elemental level.

After dinner she insisted on helping his mother clean up. His parents had a long-standing arrangement—she cooked, he cleaned. But Vernon was happy to let Piper do it, even if the look Marian sent his way promised retribution later. Mitch bit his lip and kept quiet. He could hear the women chatting about china patterns as he rose to follow his father into the den. He'd have stayed where he was and eavesdropped on their conversation if he could have—not because he particularly wanted to know what they talked about, but just to hear their voices. Listening to the two of them talking made him feel peaceful and cozy.

Why had he waited so long to start looking for someone with whom to share his life?

He didn't have any answers for that, wasn't sure they even mattered.

As soon as the two women entered the room, Piper reached for her bag. Mitch got to his feet.

"Do you have to go?" Marian asked plaintively.

"I really do, yes," Piper answered, "but thank you for a lovely dinner. It's been a pleasure meeting you."

"You're welcome any time," Vernon said, rising from his chair with one eye on the football game playing almost silently on the television screen.

"I promised to drive Piper home," Mitch announced, reaching into his pocket for the car keys.

Marian gave him a bright smile and turned to walk them out.

"We never talked about the letter," she said as they reached the front door.

"Nothing much to talk about," he told her, kissing her cheek. "I'll let you know if something informative comes up."

"All right, son. Take care. Piper, do come see us again."

"Thank you. Dinner was delicious."

"You're very welcome. Bye-bye now."

Mitch pulled open the wide Chinese-red front door, and Piper slipped out onto the low brick porch beyond.

"This is a lovely house," Piper said as she stepped down onto the brick-edged walk.

"I've always thought so. It has a kind of timeless quality about it for me."

"You know what they say. Styles change, come and go, but a classic is a classic."

"I was thinking more in relation to my childhood," he told her, guiding her toward his British-made luxury coupe parked at the crest of the shallow circular drive. "No matter how many times they redecorate, and there have been many, the house always feels the same to me. It's not even my home anymore, but *I'm* what's changed. Do you know what I mean?"

He used his remote to unlock the car doors and reached for the handle on the passenger side, which happened to be nearest.

"I'm not sure," she answered honestly, allowing him to hand her down into the leather bucket seat. "I didn't grow up in one place. My parents never even owned a home until they retired. When I think of my childhood, I think of jungles and bamboo wind chimes and being different."

He thought about that as he walked around to the driver's seat. "That must have been difficult," he said, settling in and reaching for his safety belt. Hers was already buckled. "Is that why your parents sent you away to boarding school?"

She lifted a shoulder. "I'm not sure. It may have been part of it. My feeling always was that they just wanted me to get a good education in safe surroundings, to know my home country."

"You didn't discuss it?"

She seemed to think about that. "Not really. It was always sort of a given. 'When you go back to the States for seventh grade…' It was never 'if,' always 'when.' I don't suppose I've really thought too much about it."

Obviously she had lived in a very different world from his. He started up the car and drove out to the street. While waiting for a pickup truck to pass he asked, "Would you go back to Thailand if given the opportunity?"

"To visit, of course."

"But not to live?" He turned the car into the right-hand lane.

She shook her head and after a moment said, "Somehow it was never home. Isn't that odd? I was born there, spent the first twelve years of my life so deep in the jungle that hearing English spoken openly in the halls at my school seemed weird, but something inside me always knew that it wasn't home."

"Where is home, then?" he asked, braking to a smooth halt at the stoplight on Abrams.

Several moments crept by. He'd begun to think that she wasn't going to answer when she looked at him and said, "I don't know."

He couldn't quite imagine what she meant, wasn't sure what to think or feel about such an answer. He said nothing more until he pulled into one of only four unenclosed parking spaces in front of her apartment building.

She unbuckled her belt, but before she could let herself out, he opened his own door. She subsided instantly, sinking back into her seat until he could get to his feet and move around to get her door for her. He extended a hand, and she placed her much smaller one in it.

"Every time I see you," he said as she pivoted on the seat and put her feet to the ground, "I wonder afterward why I didn't ask for your telephone number."

"Wouldn't do you any good," she said matter-of-factly.

His face must have fallen as quickly as his heart, for she suddenly smiled and said, "I don't have a telephone."

He chuckled and shook his head, crooking an arm over the edge of the open door. "I'd like to see you again."

Her gaze dropped to her toes, then rose slowly to his face. "Let's talk about it tomorrow. At lunch. In Thanksgiving Square?"

That sounded like a date to him, so he didn't quibble. If she wanted to go slowly, keep it on her terms, he could accommodate her. Nodding, he smiled and said, "Tomorrow, then."

She stepped out from behind the door. He closed it and walked beside her to the locked gate set into the grillwork of the security fence. He was glad she was sensible enough to rent in a secured building. She punched in the code, then smiled at him as the lock clicked open.

"Thank you for the ride."

He hadn't expected to be invited in, but he didn't intend to budge until that gate was locked firmly behind her. "Any time."

She went in. The gate swung shut with a clang. For a moment they just looked at each other through the heavy grillwork, then they turned and went their separate ways.

Piper woke on Monday morning wanting never to see Mitch Sayer again.

It was shocking, nonsensical, downright rude, but she couldn't help deeply regretting that they must meet. What had possessed her to suggest it? Why hadn't she realized before that he was exactly what she'd come to Dallas to escape—anything that bumped her against her past.

She prayed that it would rain, muttering for God to pour torrents down on Thanksgiving Square right through lunch, but she knew that would be only a temporary reprieve. At some point she was going to have to tell the man that she didn't want to see him again. And how would she explain that? How would she make him understand that he was too much like what she'd walked away from, too reminiscent of the old life that she absolutely had to leave behind or go mad? It would be better if she just never saw him again, but he knew where she worked and lived. He could find her if he wanted to. And he wanted to.

Sweet, merciful heaven, how had this happened?

Her father would probably say that God was testing her.

She didn't want to know what her father would say. Not that this was about abandoning her family. This was about putting together a new life, one that she could bear to live.

Maybe Mitch Sayer could live in his parents' hip pockets, but she wasn't like that. She had been reared for independence. That made her uniquely qualified for this course of action. Maybe God had always known that she would wind up on her own, far away from those dear to her, that she was going to screw up so royally that she'd have to go off, find a way to start over again. But how could she do that if every time she turned around there was Mitch Sayer making her think of all that she'd lost?

She prayed for rain, and with gut-wrenching dismay watched the sunshine glitter against the office windowpanes.

At noon, feeling belligerent and rebellious, she unzipped her sandwich bag on her desk, but when she reached for the thermos bottle of soup, her hand wouldn't quite close around it. She bowed her head and told herself that she was behaving irrationally. If she didn't want to see Mitch Sayer, no one and nothing could make her. Except...her own sense of fair play.

Angrily, reluctantly, she slapped the sandwich back into her lunch kit and snatched up the strap. Good manners could be a downright bore and a burden.

Mitch hung up the phone, jotted down a last note with his left hand, then shoved back his cuff to check the time. Three minutes past noon. Rising swiftly, he snatched his suit coat from the back of his chair and threw it on, straightening his tie as the coat settled across his shoulders. He bent and opened the bottom desk drawer to grab a folded brown paper bag. Not wanting to lose precious minutes picking up something to eat, he'd packed a lunch of sorts that morning. Bag in tow, he sailed out of the office, giving his coat pocket one last pat to make certain that his cell phone rested safely inside.

He was pleased to have received three more contacts from airline passengers. One call had given his heart a momentary jolt. The gentleman on the other end of the line had wanted to know if Mitch had found a small slip of paper—with the combination of a safe written on it. Such a slip had apparently fallen out of his wallet at some point. Mitch was sorry to disappoint him, sorrier still to be disappointed himself, but at least, after a bit of conversation, the fellow had offered Mitch the name of another traveler who might be interested in speaking to him.

The other two contacts, one a letter and one a telephone message, would take more time to follow up on, but Mitch felt encouraged to still be receiving any communications connected with the airline notice. He prayed regularly for the person who had lost the letter, but he no longer felt the sense of urgency that he had in the beginning. Urgency had been replaced by eagerness. He strode down the sidewalk with long, swift strides and a smile.

He spotted her standing beside a bench with her hands on her hips, tapping a toe. A wave of his hand sent her plopping down onto the hard stone seat. By the time he reached her side, she was munching a sandwich pensively. He dropped down beside her, abandoned his lunch bag to the vacant spot next to him and leaned close.

"What's wrong?"

She lowered the sandwich to her lap and looked up at him with stormy amber eyes that flicked back and forth across his for several seconds. Then she dropped her gaze, bowed her head and in a small voice said, "Nothing."

He didn't believe it for an instant. His hand gravitated to her back, coming to rest between her shoulder blades. She didn't seem to mind. Perhaps she didn't even realize. Perhaps his touching her felt as natural to her as it did to him.

"Rough morning?"

She nodded.

"Want to tell me about it?"

She dipped her head a little lower, but then looked up, briefly met his eyes with hers and shook her head very gently. She'd plaited only the top part of her hair that morning, leaving the braid to hang down against the thick, bright curtain of her hair in back. He thought it the most beautiful sight he'd ever seen and only just restrained himself from stroking his hand over the shiny tresses when she sighed.

"I'm just in a lousy mood."

"Let's see if we can find a little help for that," he said. Closing his eyes, he began to pray in a quiet voice. "Gracious Lord God, You have given us a glorious day, and an hour of it to spend together. We thank You for that and for this food we ask You to bless and for all the many other ways in which You show us Your love. Whenever the world beats us down, Lord, You always stand ready to pick us up again. Please lift up Piper now, Father. Let her feel Your love throughout the afternoon and always. Amen."

When he looked up again, he found her blinking a wet sheen from her eyes. An anemic smile trembled across her lips. He realized he was holding her tightly against his side; his arm had slipped around her fully at some point. She seemed to realize it at the same time and stiffened slightly.

He quickly released her, asking, "Better?"

The smile grew a little more robust. "Yes, thank you." She settled back a bit and lifted her sandwich toward her mouth. "Aren't you going to eat?"

He remembered the brown paper bag at his side. "Oh, sure."

As he pulled out hard-boiled eggs, a hunk of cheese, crackers and pickled peppers, she commented wryly, "Having your heat with a side of cholesterol, I see."

He chuckled. "The peppers aren't that hot, and my cholesterol is fine, thank you very much. I just didn't have a lot in my fridge this morning."

"I see." Her sandwich in her lap, she broke the seal on a bottle of water. "Nothing in there to drink, I take it."

He made a face, only then realizing that he'd forgotten the beverage. "Well, like I said, the peppers aren't that hot."

She produced the cap off a thermos bottle and poured water into it for herself, passing the water bottle to him. He saluted her with it.

"Thanks."

"Think nothing of it."

He thought plenty of it—and her—but he just smiled and gobbled his lunch.

Piper watched him eat the fourth boiled egg and the last of the peppers with a shake of her head.

"What?" he asked, swallowing.

"Oh, nothing. It's just that, for someone I hardly know, I sure have seen you eat a lot. This is our third meal together."

"Don't forget the other night at the restaurant. We didn't actually eat *together,* but we were in the same room."

She laughed. "Lawyers. All right, our fourth meal. Just goes to prove my point."

He shrugged and casually suggested, "Maybe we ought to find something to do together besides eat."

A thrill of expectation shot through her, and she was struck suddenly by the contradiction with her earlier feelings. Why had she thought that she wouldn't enjoy seeing him again? Something about Mitch felt comfortable and familiar; something else felt oddly compelling, if a little frightening. When she looked into his dark blue eyes she sensed the weight and significance of his experience as well as the earnestness of his emotions. The former drew her as well as repelled her; the latter tingled in her nerve endings, ephemeral, only the promise of a feeling.

But did she want that feeling? She couldn't deny that she liked him, that he *interested* her, and yet anything more seemed perilous.

Her heart pounded as she lightly tossed out a refusal. "Like I said, I hardly know you."

He sobered and softly rebutted that statement. "You know me. You already know everything important about me that there is to know."

"Do I?"

"I'm not a complicated man, Piper."

"Maybe I'm a complicated woman."

"I don't doubt it." He didn't have to say that it made no difference.

Her heart beat so hard that it hurt.

He wadded up the paper sack and seemed to ponder what to say next. When he did speak, the subject took her by surprise.

"Interesting case walked through my office door this morning."

"Oh?"

"Umm-hmm. A thirty-eight-year-old man was caught peeping in windows at women in his neighborhood."

Piper shivered. "Ugh."

Mitch nodded. "His wife was the one who caught him. She hit him eight times with a baseball bat. Broke six bones. He's in the hospital. She's in jail. Neither of them want a divorce, because they have four kids under the age of thirteen, but the D.A. wants ironclad assurance that this won't happen again if they get back together."

"Can you give him that assurance?"

"No. She's still mad enough to whack him, and he won't own up to what he did." He spread his hands in a gesture of helplessness. "They both need counseling, but of course they can't afford it. Her I can probably get into an offender's program. Him…" Mitch sighed and shook his head. "There aren't any victim's programs for what's wrong with him, even though he's more in need of help than she is. Voyeurism can be a tough addiction to break, and he won't even admit that he has a problem."

Piper shook her head, trying to work through the situation to her own satisfaction, but it was a true conundrum. The victim and the perpetrator were both guilty.

"What are you going to do?"

He sighed gustily. "Well, about the only thing I can think to do is to build a case against the husband. It's not my job. In fact, it's the exact opposite of my job, but the D.A. can't justify spending resources to do it. On the other hand, if a case is handed to him, the D.A. will file. He doesn't want a Peeping Tom on the streets any more than I do, and if I can get charges against the husband, then maybe I can get them both the help they need to put their family back together. If not, four kids are probably going to grow up in foster care."

Piper let her shoulders slump forward. "Forgive me for saying so, but that's pretty depressing."

"I think of it more as challenging," he told her, "and when a case works out well, it's downright exhilarating. I really wouldn't want to do anything else."

"I know what you mean," she said automatically, and just like that she was right back there in the emergency room, her mind racing as she assessed a patient's condition, hands flying smoothly through complicated procedures.

She felt the relieved thrill of stopping a bleed-out or feeling a heartbeat revive. She remembered the satisfaction of telling a family member that a loved one was going to make it and the defeating disappointment when it went the other way. Then compassion had become true empathy, knowledge had sharpened into actual realization and all the victories she'd ever known, all that had made her work worthwhile had turned to ashes and blown away in a puff of wind. In one awful moment she had gained real understanding and lost everything else.

The pain of it was as acute as any physical injury.

Gasping, she popped to her feet, her eyes filling with tears.

"Piper?"

She whirled away, aware that she was about to make a fool of herself, fearing much worse.

"I have to go," she choked out, shaking free of the hand that he reached out to her.

Mitch called out her name again, but she couldn't speak to him, couldn't look at him. All she wanted to do was hide. She'd run all this way to Dallas to escape the pain, and she would do it even if it meant hiding from him.

Chapter Six

Mitch looked around the mostly paved square, scanning for a bright copper head, but once again he was disappointed. He should have gone after her that day, should have insisted that she tell him what was bothering her. Whatever it was, they could work it out together—he just knew it. Provided, of course, that he ever saw her again. He'd thought about going to her apartment the previous evening, but he couldn't even get through the security gate to her apartment door. It seemed that he had only one other option, then. He set off toward the building where she worked.

Surely he was due some explanation, he told himself, striding quickly across a busy intersection and down the broad sidewalk. In reality, he just wanted to know that she was all right. She didn't have to give him an explanation if she didn't want to, so long as that bright smile was in place, so long as he could see that she was well. She didn't even have to see him again, though his stomach clenched at the thought.

He reached the front of the Medical Specialist Insurance Company building and pushed through a heavy glass door into the cool marble interior. A bank of elevators lined the opposite wall. Short leather banquettes had been fixed to the walls on either side, perpendicular to the elevators, presumably so a non-employee could sit and wait for a friend or family member to come down. Every elevator but one required an electronic pass card, and it was clearly marked "Visitors." Mitch walked to it and punched the up button set into the marble. The doors slid open instantly.

He stepped into the car. The doors closed, and the elevator began to rise even as Mitch realized that there were no more buttons to push, no choice of floors to be made. The Medical Specialist Insurance Company was obviously careful to protect its workspace and employees from unwanted intrusion. He supposed they had to be.

As swiftly as it had risen, the elevator car stopped, and the doors disappeared. Mitch strode into a large room fashioned into a maze of modular cubicles and cordoned off by a half wall of wood, behind which a trio of receptionists sat, all with headphones and mouthpieces. A brisk older woman was talking on the telephone, while a stylish younger one carefully wrote something in a padded book. A reed-thin kid, maybe still in high school and wearing a blindingly white shirt and tightly knotted necktie, waved Mitch over.

"Can I help you?"

"Yes, I'd like to see Ms. Wynne, Ms. Piper Wynne." Mitch turned away, hoping to forestall any questions, but the company had trained their employees well.

"I'll need you to sign my register," the young man said, sliding a padded volume to the edge of the half wall. A pen was attached to the spine via a beaded chain.

Mitch quickly scrawled his name, wrote "attorney" in the space requiring an occupation and "personal" under the column demanding to know his business. The kid turned the book and glanced over the entry, then looked up a number and punched it into a hidden keypad. After a few seconds he spoke.

"Mr. Mitchell Sayer, attorney, to see Ms. Wynne. Umm-hmm. Umm-hmm. I'll tell him." The *boy*—he didn't look as if he could possibly shave—broke the connection and fixed Mitch with a no-arguments stare. "Ms. Wynne is out."

Mitch tamped down his irritation. "Out for lunch? Because I can wait if I have to."

"Out for the day," the young fellow said, hitting the last word hard for emphasis. "Maybe longer."

"She's not ill, is she?"

The other fellow didn't so much as blink. "Not that I'm aware of."

Mitch's stomach sank. He thought briefly of leaving a message, but he figured that she'd already gotten it and sent one of her own. Hers said, "Go away."

He looked at his feet, nodded brusquely and turned toward the elevator with a muttered "Thanks."

Once safely inside the silent car, he closed his eyes and let disappointment unfurl inside him. He was in his office and at his desk before he could tell himself that he obviously wasn't meant to be more than a passing acquaintance to Piper Wynne.

All right. So be it.

He didn't like it, but what difference did that make? He would just have to focus his attention elsewhere. God had something, someone, for him. He could think about other matters, other purposes. Such as the letter.

There was one contact in Houston with whom Mitch had not yet spoken. The fellow had responded late last week to the airline's notification, and he and Mitch had been playing telephone tag for several days. Mitch had been the last one to leave a message, but hey, he thought, might as well try again now.

Lifting the telephone receiver from its cradle, he dialed the number, reading it off the notepad at his elbow, then sat back in his chair and waited for the familiar sound of an answering machine. What he got instead was the man himself.

"Well, hello, there," he said pleasantly, his mood lightening somewhat. "This is Mitchell Sayer calling."

"Oh, Mr. Sayer!" the man said, recognizing his name at once. "I'm so sorry I haven't gotten back to you." He went on to tell Mitch that at first he'd dismissed the notice the airline had sent, then later had realized that he'd misplaced an important letter. Mitch sat up abruptly.

"A letter, you say?"

"A very important letter. I was frantic for a few days. I'd kept the airline notice—I generally keep everything—and it did say an item of no *actual* value, so I gave you a call on the off chance—"

In his excitement, Mitch interrupted. "Can you describe the letter for me, sir?"

"It was a letter of intent. Being an attorney, I'm sure you're familiar with the term."

Mitch *was* familiar with the term, familiar enough to know that this man's letter was *not* the letter in Mitch's possession. Deflated, he barely heard the rest of what was being said—something about a large company buying out a smaller one. He waited for a lull in the flow of words, then gave the bad news.

"I'm sorry, but I didn't recover your letter."

"Oh, I know that," the man said, unperturbed. "I found it filed improperly. My secretary has a bad habit of picking up things off my desk and putting them away for me, as if just having them out of sight clears up the business."

Mitch found a pallid smile. "I see."

"I've had a strong talk with her about this," the fellow went on, "and I meant to call you yesterday to let you know that I'm not the person you're looking for. Sorry I didn't get to it."

"That's okay. I'm glad you found your letter. I just wish I could find whoever lost the one I have in my possession. You, um, didn't happen to see anyone else drop a small folded sheet of paper while moving down the loading ramp to the airplane that day, did you?"

"Well," the man said, "I sure didn't, but maybe one of our group did. I could ask them to call you or just give you their names and numbers—whatever you prefer."

Mitch perked up. "You don't think they'd mind talking to me?"

"Not at all, but there were about a half dozen of us. If you'd rather not make that many calls—"

"No!" Mitch said quickly. "That's fine. I don't mind at all."

"Just let me get those numbers, then."

Mitch closed his eyes while he waited for the gentleman to get back on the line. Things were looking up, he assured himself. Surely one of these folks saw something pertinent or could at least lead him to someone else who had.

Holding the phone between his right ear and shoulder, he prepared to write down this new list of leads. It was a little like looking up and seeing a light at the end of a long, dark tunnel. He suspected it was a holy light, and he thanked God for it.

He had come to the office looking for her.

She tried not to think about it, tried not to think about him at all. That way she didn't have to remember running away in a panic with tears threatening to spill down her cheeks. It was exactly that kind of humiliating behavior that she was trying to put behind her, and she had been correct in assuming that Mitch Sayer was a stumbling block along her path toward that goal.

She didn't know why, really, but something about him put her in direct touch with her past. Houston and all that had happened there seemed distant and misty unless she was with him. What was he—some spiritual or metaphysical conduit to her most painful moments? She shivered at the thought, but more mystifying still was how relaxed and comfortable she felt in his company, until the memories blindsided her.

It was a pity, because she really did like the man, but she just couldn't be with him and preserve her sanity.

She leaned over the side of the chaise and trailed her fingers in the water. It was still warm enough to swim in the afternoon, but the evening was too cool. She liked the serenity here when there was no one else to splash and laugh and scrape the furniture across the decking.

"Oh, for pity's sake," Melissa said, breaking into Piper's reverie. Piper had almost forgotten she was there, sitting next to a glass-topped table with an open novel in her lap.

"What?" Piper asked, assuming that the slightly sarcastic outburst had something to do with what Melissa was reading.

"You!" Melissa replied, to Piper's shock.

"Me?"

"Yes, you. What has got you so down?"

Piper laughed lightly, as if to prove her friend wrong. "I'm not down."

"And I'm not human," Melissa retorted dryly.

Piper fixed her with a deadpan look. "I knew there was something fishy about you."

"Right. I'm a fish, and you're as happy as a pig in clover."

"I am *not* depressed," Piper insisted. "I'm just bored."

"Okay, fine." Melissa set aside her book. "Let's go out and have a little fun, then."

Piper smiled perkily. "Excellent."

"I'll have Scott call Nate."

Piper's face fell before she could stop her reaction. "Uh, let's not."

"He wants to see you again."

Piper controlled her grimace. Barely. "It wouldn't be fair. Nate's not my type, and even if he were, I don't want to see any one person right now. I want to keep my options open, you know?''

Melissa shrugged. ''Is that why you aren't seeing that Mitch guy?''

Piper's gaze sharpened. ''What made you think I would be?''

''Maybe it was the way you perked up when you laid eyes on him at the restaurant that night,'' Melissa said, ''or the way you gushed afterward about meeting him.''

''I'm not seeing Mitch,'' Piper said flatly.

''Duh,'' Melissa said. ''If you were, would you be sitting here with me on a Saturday evening? I think not.''

''I—I just…''

''Want to keep your options open,'' Melissa said dryly. ''Hey, it's okay by me, but if you really want to look over the options, why don't we go hear this band down at the West End?''

Piper squirmed inwardly. She'd never been one to frequent concerts, but what else did she have to do? Besides, it might be fun just to see what went on. She could listen to some music, do a little people watching. What could it hurt?

''I'm, uh, not sure I have anything to wear.''

Melissa flopped a hand dismissively at that. ''Oh, we can come up with something.'' She scooted forward to the edge of her chair, hands on the arms, ready to rise. ''Why don't I run it by Scott, and if he's up for it, I'll come down, and we'll take a look in your closet. Okay?''

Smiling, Piper squelched a niggle of dismay. ''Sure.''

Melissa lunged to her feet, proclaiming eagerly, "I'm going to wear spandex!"

Piper's spirits sank even lower. "If Scott doesn't want to go, don't press him," she said hopefully. "We can always do it another time."

"Oh, he'll want to," Melissa promised, hurrying away. She looked back over her shoulder. "He loves the band that's playing."

Piper closed her eyes and tried to tell herself that she wouldn't be sorry.

The music pulsated so loudly that Piper felt sure the walls must bulge with each thunderous beat. Melissa and Scott seemed to have perfected a style of communication for just such deafening circumstances, including hand gestures, well-aimed shouts and a form of lipreading that involved exaggerated pronunciations. For her part, Piper felt lost in a world of chaotic noise and shifting shadows peopled with slightly threatening bodies. She found it impossible even to enjoy people watching at these decibels. To say that she was out of her element was putting it mildly. She looked around and wondered if she were even part of the same species as these laughing shrieking creatures.

When the wildly energetic band finally took a break, she realized that her ears were ringing and perhaps always would. Scott bounced up to journey to the concession area for fresh sodas and a gratis basket of popcorn salty enough to guarantee an increase in beverage sales. Piper had been careful to limit herself to ginger ale, prompting Scott to jokingly proclaim her a "cheap date." When he offered her another refill she declined with a smile and shake of her head, then studiously pretended not to notice the activities around their tiny, cramped table.

The room was dark, but not so dark that she couldn't see those around her. She fixed her attention on a raucous group at the bar, only to realize within moments that the hilarity was being generated by a contest among the males. They were launching kernels of popcorn up into the air and trying to swallow them. Piper looked away, only to start when someone bumped her chair from behind.

She glanced over her shoulder, just as that someone began telling a joke to someone out of sight.

"So there's this guy on a deserted island, just him and the birdies for months on end, when one day three women wash ashore, a blond, a brunette and a redhead...."

Piper tried to tune him out, but he was practically standing on top of her, and as the story grew more ribald by the syllable, she felt her cheeks begin to burn. Squirming in her chrome-and-plastic chair, she sought mightily for a way to shut out the words. She even began to wish for the earsplitting music to crank up again, despite the continued ringing in her ears. Seeing her discomfort, Melissa made a valiant attempt to come to her rescue.

"I really like that coppery orange on you. It makes your eyes positively glow."

Piper smiled. "Thank you."

It wasn't the best conversational gambit. Melissa had gushed about the stretchy knit top from the moment she'd pulled it from Piper's closet earlier that evening, and she'd repeated that bit about the eyes three times already. Nevertheless, any distraction was greatly appreciated at this point—not that it helped much. As the punch line drew near—hopefully—the jokester actually raised his voice, launching Piper into desperate conversation.

"I wish I could wear that shade of red you have on," she said so loudly that Melissa looked pained.

It was Piper's turn to wince as the joke reached its punch line, employing a certain expression she found particularly vile. Even Melissa's cheeks pinked. As laugher erupted around them, Melissa leaned across the table.

"This isn't really your scene, is it?"

Piper blanched guiltily. "I guess not, but that doesn't mean I'm not enjoying myself. The band seems good."

Melissa slanted a pitying look at her. "They are, but the music's too loud even for me. I'll ask Scott to take us home when he gets back to the table."

Piper felt immense relief, but good manners made her voice a token protest. "Oh, you don't have to do that. I don't want to ruin anyone's evening, and he seems to be enjoying himself."

Melissa flipped a hand nonchalantly. "Don't worry about that. We can come back another time. It'll be more fun a few weeks from now, anyway. These new clubs always start out trying to blow you out of the room, show you they've got the necessary ingredients for a good time, you know?"

"They certainly have the necessary sound equipment," Piper commented wryly, "provided, of course, that a good time necessitates rendering one permanently deaf."

Melissa chuckled. "They'll tone it down some before long."

As far as Piper was concerned, they could tone it down a lot and still be too loud.

Scott returned a few minutes later, and Piper was glad to see that he'd almost finished his soda already, if not the basket of popcorn that he placed in the center of the tiny table. Immediately Melissa rose, wrapped her arms around his neck and whispered into his ear. He grinned and quickly downed the remainder of the liquid in his glass, wrapped an arm around his wife's slender waist and happily abandoned the basket of popcorn as he stood.

"What are we waiting for?"

Piper telegraphed her friend a silent message of thanks as they began winding their way toward the door. As they stepped down onto the relatively peaceful sidewalk, Melissa linked arms with her husband, gave Piper a wink and set off at a brisk pace toward the lot where they'd left their small, foreign-made, economy coupe.

Once at the car, Piper crawled into the narrow back seat and belted herself in. Melissa and Scott dropped into the front buckets, with Melissa behind the wheel, and they were shortly off. As they drove swiftly through the busy, darkened Dallas streets, Scott kept his hand on his wife's knee, occasionally giving it a squeeze. Melissa would shoot him a smile every so often and get a rub or a pat in return. Piper pretended not to notice.

She had never felt quite so alone.

Once the car was parked in its narrow assigned space at the apartment house and they had all managed to climb out without denting those automobiles occupying spots on either side, Piper thanked her friends for the evening and started toward the rear pass-through into the inner courtyard. Scott and Melissa followed. Piper didn't have to look to know that Scott had his arms wrapped around his wife, but as the trio drew near the bottom of the stairs Melissa disengaged and sent Scott on ahead, promising to be right up after walking Piper to her door.

Piper put her off. "Don't be silly. I'm ten feet from home. Go on up with your husband."

Melissa reached for Piper's hand, her warm hazel eyes intent. "Not until I'm sure that you're okay. What is it, hon? It's pretty clear to me that something's bothering you."

To Piper's dismay, she felt the hot weight of sudden tears behind her eyes. To hide them, she employed a slight laugh and gave her head a little shake.

"Can't fool you, can I? It's just a headache. I didn't want to complain. The loud music and all...you know how it is."

"Are you sure it's just a headache?" Melissa asked, her voice tinged with concern.

Piper knew it was more than that, but evaded the question. "I'll be okay tomorrow. You go on up to your husband, and don't worry about me."

"If you're sure," Melissa hedged uncertainly.

Piper squeezed her friend's hand and pulled free. "Go on. If I'm not mistaken, you have promises to keep."

Melissa grinned. "Oh, yeah." She waggled an eyebrow and swung around the end of the heavy metal banister up onto the stairs. "See you tomorrow," she called, pelting up the steps.

Piper smiled and waved before turning desperately toward her own door and safe haven.

Melissa and Scott seemed so happy together, so

crazy about each other, and she was delighted for them, but she couldn't help thinking how shallow and pointless her own life seemed to be. Was this what God intended for her? she wondered bitterly. Was this her punishment, to forever feel out of sync and alone despite such friendship? Tears were streaming down her face by the time she got inside the apartment, and this time she couldn't seem to stop them.

Chapter Seven

Mitch wasn't looking for her, not really, or so he told himself as he stood staring down at the busy sidewalk. The plate-glass window of his office offered a great view of the insurance building where she worked. It was just past noon, and he had been standing here fully ten minutes or more, craning his head, cheek almost touching the glass. He had performed this same ritual the previous Thursday and Friday, since he'd visited her office and been so obviously rebuffed. Why couldn't he get it through his head that she didn't want to see him?

Accept it, counselor, he told himself sternly, but even as he thought the words, he spied a bright, pale copper head behind the glass doors of the Medical Specialist building facade. His breath stopped, and his heart began to race when she pushed through to the sidewalk. She paused for a moment, glanced down the street in his direction, tugged on the tie of the heavy sweater belted at her waist and turned toward the square, her lunch kit in one hand.

Mitch didn't think about whether or not he should follow her. He didn't have to. The decision had been made long ago without his even realizing it, and he was of no mind to second-guess. Grabbing his suit coat from the hanger inside the small closet, he tore out of his office. His eyes barely registered the full wall of built-in amenities—from sink, small refrigerator, television set and file cabinets.

He hadn't brought his lunch, but he wasn't concerned about that just now. His secretary had left earlier, and when he'd told her that he wouldn't be going out, she'd offered to bring back something for him to eat. She would most likely return before him, but he didn't bother leaving her a note to let her know where to find him. All that mattered at the moment was getting to the square before Piper left it, provided of course that was where she was going. At this point, he wasn't taking anything for granted.

Hurrying along the sidewalk, he told God silently that he wasn't trying to circumvent His will, that he would accept it without question if she wasn't where he hoped to find her, but he also didn't hesitate to ask that she be there. His pulse was racing more than necessary when he reached the square. Pausing, he shaded his eyes against the autumn sun—he'd forgotten his shades in his haste—and surveyed the area. She was sitting on one end of a concrete ledge on the other side of the square. He almost dropped with relief.

Thank You. Thank You. Thank You.

He pulled a deep breath, slipped his hands into the pockets of his pants and strolled toward her with a studied nonchalance that he certainly didn't feel. He was halfway across the square when she looked up, turned her head and spotted him. She didn't acknowledge his presence in any way, but she didn't get up and leave, either; as he drew near, she lifted her gaze from her sandwich to his face again and nodded. Even though her usual smile was missing, he tried not to let it bother him, but his greeting was tentative nonetheless.

"Hello."

"Hello." She looked back to her sandwich, undecided for a moment, and then grimly bit off a small piece of it. He wandered closer. Chewing, she slid down a little, though there were yards of room on the wide ledge. She swallowed and said, "Have a seat."

Wary of spooking her into flight again, Mitch tried not to let his pleasure or hopefulness show as he hitched a leg up onto the ledge and scooted into place. They were actually sitting on top of a low wall that shielded the steps leading down into the underground passageways linking some of the downtown buildings. She almost had her back to him, but not enough to prevent his joining her.

He realized suddenly that he hadn't thought at all about what he was going to say to her because he hadn't really expected to see her again. Making a quick decision, he ignored all that had happened before—her running away and then avoiding him—in favor of simple pleasantries.

"How have you been?" Okay, not so simple, perhaps.

"All right," she said, not looking at him.

He took that at face value. She wasn't fine, she wasn't awful, she was just okay.

"Me, too," he replied, adding, "Busy, as usual."

She adjusted her seat on the cold concrete and nibbled at her sandwich. "What happened with your Peeping Tom?"

He savored her interest for a moment before answering. "He pleaded guilty to a minor offense after one of his victims decided to press charges."

Piper cut him a wry, knowing glance. "Did you have a hard time talking her into it?"

His grin flashed before he could stop it. "Nope."

She disciplined a smile and arched a fine brow. "Is it enough to get your client the counseling he needs?"

"My client's husband, actually, and yes, it is. His court-appointed attorney made it a condition of his probation."

She turned her head, fixing him with an appreciative stare. "And was *that* difficult for you to arrange?"

He tried not to feel smug or prideful. "It was, actually. The court probably would have doled out probation without counseling if his lawyer hadn't asked for it, but I managed to convince her to fill out the paperwork and chase down the necessary signatures."

Piper hitched a shoulder contemplatively. "What did you have to promise her?"

"Nothing much—just the usual quid pro quo."

Piper shifted so that she was facing forward, and he silently admired her profile: sleek head, thick hair plaited flat against her skull revealing one dainty ear, then hanging loose from her nape to the bottoms of her shoulder blades. He appreciated her smooth forehead, the slight indentation of a wide, almond-shaped eye fringed with glinting copper-gold lashes, the delicate bridge and tilt-tipped nub of her nose and the lush contours of her full mouth. Her slightly pointed chin seemed to lack its usual stubborn jut.

He wanted to put his arms around her, tell her that everything was going to be fine, for he knew without doubt that she was deeply troubled. He assumed that such an embrace would be unwelcome, though. She sighed, looking so unbearably forlorn that he almost put that assumption to the test.

Then she shocked him by saying, "I'm a nurse, you know, not a glorified clerk." She put her head down. "Guess I'm having a difficult time making the adjustment to the new job."

A nurse. He'd thought that insurance had always been her field. Then again, lots of nurses worked for insurance companies in managed care. He cleared his throat and gathered his thoughts.

"I take it you worked with patients before."

She nodded and looked down at the sandwich she obviously didn't want. "I've always worked in a hospital until now." She tossed him a wry smile that didn't have much besides irony in it. "I thought this would be a good change of pace."

"But you miss the old job," he surmised.

She laid aside her sandwich with a grimace. "Frankly, reviewing cases is a bore."

"It's important, though. You're still making a genuine contribution."

"Am I? I don't know."

"Then why not go back to what you love? The hospitals around here are always looking for help."

She shook her head firmly. "No."

That didn't make a lot of sense to him. "Look," he argued gently, "if the new job isn't a good fit, then just change."

"Maybe I haven't given it enough time," she said

listlessly. "Besides, it wouldn't look good on my résumé—leaving after only a few weeks."

"So stick with it awhile longer, then go back," he suggested.

She looked away as if scrutinizing a distant future—or was it the past? Then she abruptly dropped her gaze to her lap.

"We'll see."

She seemed so sad that he took a chance by reaching for her hand. Gratified when she didn't immediately pull away, he clasped it in both of his.

"If it makes you feel any better, I'm going to pray for you regularly from now on."

Her smile trembled. "Thank you, Mitch. That's very kind after…" Biting her lip, she ducked her head. "It's not you," she told him softly. "It's me. It's always been me."

"Don't worry about it," he said gently.

She tilted her head back, gulping air as if trying to keep tears at bay.

"I'm going to stop feeling sorry for myself," she muttered fiercely. "I am absolutely going to stop this."

He chuckled in sympathy. "I find that a little distraction helps."

"Oh?" she returned lightly. Then she added, "What would you suggest?"

His heart thumped, kicking his brain into high gear. She had opened a door, through which he was quite eager to carefully pass.

"Uh, music." Yes, that was good. He knew a little something of her tastes. "I have tickets to the Meyerson Symphony Center Tuesday performances."

He didn't. What he meant was that his parents had a subscription and he often, sometimes, went in one or the other's place. He felt sure that they'd give up both seats for a good cause, and he certainly couldn't think of a better one than this. He didn't bother explaining all that to Piper, though, and as it turned out, he didn't have to.

Her face lit with the first genuine smile he'd seen from her today, and her hand flexed between his. "That sounds wonderful!"

He laughed. "It is. I mean, it will be—if you'll go with me."

She leaned in a bit, a glimmer of the Piper with whom he'd become familiar, and confided teasingly, "I did assume that you were inviting me."

"Absolutely." He couldn't stop grinning. It was altogether too obvious of him, but he just couldn't help himself.

She cocked her head inquiringly, then after a moment asked, "What time?"

"Ah!" He felt like the biggest dolt around. "I should pick you up, oh, about seven-thirty. Tomorrow evening. I did say that, didn't I—Tuesday?"

She grinned. "You did, yes. So tomorrow evening at half past seven."

"Unless you want to go to dinner first?"

She laughed. "Eating again."

He remembered what she'd said before about sharing so many meals, given the relatively short amount of time they'd spent together. "Right."

She wrinkled her nose. "Let's skip it. I mean, by the time I can get home from work it'll be going on six, and I want to have time to dress. It's not formal, is it?"

"Oh, no. Semi, at best. Some folks show up in their jeans." He shrugged, adding, "Wear whatever you like."

"I'm correct in assuming that you won't show up in your jeans, aren't I?"

"Only if you want me to."

She shook her head. "You tell me what you usually wear."

He shrugged. "Suit."

"And tie?"

"Not always. Sometimes I wear a pullover under my jacket."

"Okay," she said. "I'll be appropriately dressed and waiting at half past seven."

"Better make it seven," he said on second thought, "if that gives you enough time. I want to find a good parking spot. Otherwise, we could be all night getting out of the lot."

"I can manage seven," she agreed readily. "Oh, and I'd better give you the code to the security gate."

Mitch smiled. "All right."

She recited the sequence of numbers, which he instantly committed to memory. He repeated them back to her.

"That's it," she confirmed, adding playfully, "You're my first breach of security."

Mitch felt for a moment as if he could walk on air. Then she pulled her hand from his, picked up her sandwich and remarked that the weather was unusually fine today.

"Never seen finer," he told her honestly, remarking silently that this might well be the best day in recent memory.

Mclissa helped her dress for the evening. She insisted that Piper wear the long-sleeved, form-fitting orange top. They settled on a slender, ankle-length black skirt and a long black scarf to go with it. Accompanied by black, wedge-heeled shoes, matching stockings and a silver chain with a turquoise pendant, the outfit seemed stylish, even dramatic, without being overly dressy.

They wrangled over her hair, but Melissa won in the end, simply because they ran out of time. After laboring for what seemed like hours, Melissa had just pronounced her chignon complete when the doorbell rang. Melissa went to answer it while Piper took a final look at the twisted and coiled mass from which tendrils drifted artfully, one long tress snaking from its very center. It was much more elaborate than her usual confining braid, and a tad trendy for her taste, but it would have to do.

She sighed with resignation even as she heard Melissa introduce herself while letting in Mitch. His deep voice replied, and Piper was aware of a fluttery feeling in the pit of her stomach.

She briefly closed her eyes in a bid for courage, wondering again if she had made the right decision. His invitation had seemed like a Godsend yesterday in the square, an opportunity to get her life back on a familiar, even keel, and yet she was all too aware that Mitch Sayer represented some danger to her. What that was she could not exactly determine, and truthfully she almost didn't care any longer.

Life had somehow gotten ridiculously complicated, and she wanted relief in a half-comfortable form. Any danger that he represented seemed a suitable price to pay for an evening of sedate classical music. At least she wouldn't have to worry about going deaf from the experience!

Leaving her tiny bathroom, she swept a small black leather handbag from atop her rented dresser and strode into the living area. Mitch stood with his back to her, his hands in the pants pockets of his expensive black suit as he conversed with Melissa.

"That's the beauty of a small apartment house," he was saying. "The neighbors get to know one another."

Before Melissa could reply, he turned to greet Piper.

"Ready as I'm ever going to be," she announced, too nervous to let herself register his expression. Instead, she fiddled with the chain strap on her handbag, settling it on one shoulder, then checked the lay of the scarf, which she had simply draped around her neck in front, leaving the long ends to dangle down her back.

Belatedly, she realized that the room had quietened into an unnatural silence. Glancing up, she caught Melissa's eye. Folding her arms smugly, her friend lifted an eyebrow and gave her head a slight nod in Mitch's direction. Piper steeled herself and pivoted. He stood there in the middle of her floor with his mouth open, one hand resting on the front of the sleek, ice-blue pullover under his suit coat.

"I think you knocked his eyeballs right out of his head," Melissa muttered.

"Umm." Mitch grinned sheepishly in agreement.

Piper rolled her eyes, but she was smiling. "I guess I look okay, then, huh?"

"No," he said, quietly serious, "you look stunning."

Her smile widened. "Stunning? Really?"

His gaze swept her appreciatively. "And then some."

"Why, thank you."

Melissa made a show of buffing her fingernails on her sleeve. "My work here is done."

Laughing, Piper crossed the room to kiss her friend's cheek. "Get out of here before your head swells up so big you can't force it through the door."

"The door wouldn't dare get in my way," Melissa joked dramatically, dancing to it and pulling it open. "Now, remember, children, the coach turns back into a pumpkin at midnight."

"Yes, fairy godmother," Piper said, tongue in cheek. "Thank you, fairy godmother. *Goodbye,* fairy godmother."

"Ta," Melissa said, fluttering her fingers at them as she pulled the door closed.

Piper laughed. Mitch just shook his head. "Honestly, you look beautiful."

"Honestly, I thank you."

"I mean, you always look beautiful," he amended, "but tonight especially so." Then he offered his arm. "Shall we?"

Piper slipped her hand around the crook of his elbow, quipping, "Those parking spaces are filling up as we speak."

"Funny, I don't really care anymore," he said as he led her toward the door. "I think I'd like being stuck in a parking garage with you. Or anywhere else, for that matter."

She didn't know what to say to that, so she just ducked her head and let herself be swept out into the courtyard.

* * *

The Meyerson was a wonder, an architectural and acoustical jewel with all the finest amenities. Seated comfortably in the eleventh row, with Mitch at her side, Piper felt a certain reverence in the great hall. People spoke in hushed, respectful tones even as they shifted to and fro in search of seats and companions. Mitch was right about one seeing every mode of dress, from cowboy hat and boots to the understated tuxedo. The majority, however, were dressed as she and Mitch were. Piper had never felt more attractive or more eager for an evening of Mendelssohn and Mozart.

The music was breathtaking. She had never experienced a full, live professional orchestra before, and from the moment the musicians began to tune their instruments, Piper was enraptured.

"Now, this is more my speed," she murmured in the midst of the first selection, wondering how she had ever let herself be talked into nightclub-variety rock music.

Mitch bent his head to hers, whispering, "Did you say something?"

"It's wonderful," she told him softly. "I'm so glad you asked me."

He folded her hand in his. "Makes two of us."

During the break she had to be coaxed to stand and stretch her legs, but she didn't want to leave her seat even for the promise of drinks in the beautiful lobby. A few others seemed of like mind, though most crowded the aisles, surging toward the concessions.

A small, elderly man accompanied by a child rose from the seat in front of them, stretched and turned to greet Mitch with a handshake. Outfitted in a tuxedo that had seen better days, not to mention a better fit, he wore a dapper blue bow tie, presumably to match his eyes.

"Mitchell." He ogled Piper openly, craning his balding head around rather stiffly. "I see that you're not with one of your parents this evening."

"No, sir. Not tonight."

"And for good reason, it would appear."

Mitch's mouth quirked with a grin. "Very good. Allow me to introduce her. Mr. Ivan Sontag, meet Miss Piper Wynne."

The elderly gentleman took her hand in his own gnarled one and lifted it almost to his mouth, bowing over it in a very courtly manner. "My pleasure, Miss Wynne."

"Thank you."

"Your name inspired by the bird, I take it?"

"It is, yes."

"Well, then, you have something in common with my great-grandson here, Robin Sontag Phillips." He nudged the sloe-eyed child with the lank, slicked-back hair. "Make your greeting, Robin. Remember what Papa has taught you?"

The boy displayed all the characteristics of Down's syndrome. Sweetly compliant, he folded an arm across his middle and bobbed a bow. Piper smiled.

"Hello, Robin."

"How *do* you *do*." He looked up at his great-grandfather expectantly and received a pat as reward.

"You're looking very handsome tonight, Robin," Mitch complimented, taking in the smartly tailored tux and pin-tucked shirt.

The child beamed. "Thank you."

"I especially like the red bow tie."

Robin stroked the red silk proudly, then he pointed at Piper. "Her hair's pretty."

"Why, thank you, Robin," Piper said.

"I have a girlfriend," he announced with a giggle.

Ivan Sontag chuckled and gathered his great-grandchild close to his side. "She's a very pretty little thing, too," he said affectionately.

"Papa spoils me," Robin confessed happily.

"And you spoil Papa," the old man returned, prompting the boy to clasp his arms about the elder's waist.

"Papa's old," the boy stated baldly. "He's ninety!"

"We're ninety and nine," Ivan said with a wink, "a perfect combination."

"I have to go to the bathroom," Robin declared, suddenly pulling away and dancing in place.

Sontag sighed. "All right, all right." He was smiling as he ushered the child up the aisle.

"Quite a charming pair," Piper commented, retaking her seat. "Mr. Sontag is awfully spry for ninety."

Mitch folded himself down beside her. "Do you recognize the name?" he asked.

It did seem oddly familiar, but she shook her head.

"Sontag diamonds?"

Her eyes rounded. She'd seen the billboards and the glossy magazine advertisements. "Really?"

Mitch nodded. "Very old money and lots of it. His grandson-in-law runs the business now, I understand."

"Robin's father?"

"Yes. The boy lives with Ivan, though."

"Oh? Why is that?"

Mitch crossed his legs and brushed lint from the

thigh of his trousers. "His parents are...not pleased to have a Down's syndrome child. They prefer to concentrate on their two *normal* children."

Piper felt her heart turn over in her chest. "Poor Robin."

"Oh, no," Mitch corrected. "He's a very wealthy child. Ivan saw to it after his son died in a small airplane crash some years ago. It seems that Robin was the only family member *not* mentioned in some way in his grandfather's will."

Piper shook her head. "What's going to happen to him after Mr. Sontag goes?"

"He'll own a mansion in Highland Park, be attended by a board of executors, live at the finest schools with the finest doctors in Switzerland, along with his longtime nanny and caretaker."

"And for all that he'll be alone," Piper said pensively.

"I'm afraid so," Mitch agreed.

What fools, Piper thought, to abandon one's own family. She felt her skin grow cold suddenly as a heretofore unacknowledged truth hit her squarely between the eyes. If Robin's parents and grandparents were fools, then she had to include herself among them. Perhaps Robin's family had abandoned him, but she had abandoned her whole family. There really was no other way to describe it; she saw that now. Yet, what could be done about it?

Mitch shifted beside her, and she told herself sternly that this was not the time to try to think things through. Instead, she made an attempt to shake off the melancholy. An instant later she felt Mitch's arm settle about her shoulders.

"Cold?"

"It is a little chilly in here," she mumbled, feeling his warmth with a shock of realization.

He snuggled her close to his side, smiling down at her. "Better?"

It was. Indeed it was. So much so that her heart crawled up to lodge in her throat. She laid her head on his shoulder, as much to hide her confusion as to enjoy the heat, comfort and shelter of his big, solid body.

How could it be, she wondered, that the one man who most troubled her was also the one who most put her at ease and made her feel safe?

Chapter Eight

Had she thought him dangerous? She couldn't imagine why. On the other hand, there was much that she didn't know about him. She cleared her throat.

"Can I ask you something?"

"Anything."

She pondered where to begin. "How old are you?"

"Thirty-eight. You?"

"Twenty-six."

"I knew you were young."

She lifted her head at that. "I'm not young. Melissa's young. I'm…not young."

"I didn't say *too* young."

"Oh."

He gently pushed her head back down upon his shoulder, and she left it there for a moment while she tried to puzzle out her own reactions. Sometimes she simply didn't understand herself. How, then, could she even hope to understand him? All she knew was that she wanted to.

"Can I ask you something else?"

"Same answer as the first time."

She rolled her eyes upward, gazing at the strong line of his jaw. "Why have you never remarried?"

He lifted his hand and brushed a tendril of hair from her cheek, prompting her to lift her head and meet his velvet-blue gaze.

"I guess I've been waiting for God to bring the right woman into my life," he said carefully.

Piper gulped. Her? Was he considering *her* as that woman?

His eyes, a smoky blue now, seemed to say so.

Her heart stopped, only to pick up again at double speed when his hand rested on her cheek.

"I want to kiss you," he confessed softly. "I've wanted to kiss you for a long time. At a more appropriate moment, may I?"

The irises of his eyes were ringed now with a thin line the same shade of blue as that at the base of a flame, hot enough to scorch, to steal the air from her lungs. She couldn't get enough breath to answer him, so she simply nodded. Smiling, he pressed her head back down onto his shoulder and linked his hands, bringing both arms around her.

He wanted to kiss her, had asked permission to kiss her. She had half believed that he felt sorry for her, but no! That was her feeling sorry for herself. He just wanted, was waiting, for someone to love. How could she think that it might be her? How could he? Her head swirled. All the butterflies in the universe fluttered around inside her.

He wasn't just dangerous, this man. He was lethal!

And she didn't care—couldn't, somehow, even with everything a mess, her life upside down and inside out, the past an open gash in her heart.

Oh, God, help me, she thought, and she didn't even know why—couldn't find words for what she was asking. But wasn't that the problem? She had been in over her head so long that she didn't even know which way was up, and now here was Mitchell Sayer, towing her by the hand, but in which direction? Not that it mattered anymore. Without him she was lost. Perhaps even with him she was lost, but at least she wasn't alone—not for now, anyway.

She turned her face into the curve of his neck and for the first time in a very long while let herself just be. She would worry about the mess she'd made of her life later. For now it was enough just to be with Mitch.

Presently the house lights flickered and began to lower. The audience and musicians quickly returned to their positions. Robin and Mr. Sontag were among the last, escorted by a uniformed usher who shone a tiny light on the floor, to mark their way along the darkened aisle. No sooner were they in their seats than the program began. Just as the welcoming applause died away and the maestro lifted his baton, Robin turned to hiss a giggling explanation at Piper and Mitch.

"The line was very long! I almost wet myself!"

The man next to Piper shushed the child curtly. Piper glared at him, but Mr. Sontag whispered to Robin, and the boy turned dutifully toward the stage, flashing a little smile at Piper. That smile seemed to say, "You and I know I'm special." And so he was. In fact, Piper reflected, everything about this evening was special.

She laid her head back against Mitch's arm and stared up at the high ceiling, letting the music wash over her in lush waves of pure beauty. She felt at peace, adrift on a sea of calm, and yet keenly aware of the strong arms about her, the solid body at her side.

He wanted to kiss her.

She must not have mucked up her life so terribly badly after all. Perhaps one day she'd look around and find that all the monsters had vanished.

The end of the program came as a surprise to Piper. It seemed only moments had passed since the intermission. Yet people were getting to their feet, Mitch included, to applaud. He lifted her up with him as he rose, one arm tucking neatly around her back, his hand at her waist. Piper tried to clap appreciatively enough for both of them. The applause seemed to last longer than the performance, with the maestro taking bow after bow.

Finally it was over. The audience moved into the aisles, speaking and laughing in low tones. With some concern Piper saw that Sontag and his great-grandson had managed to get into the throng ahead of them. Robin clutched Ivan's hand almost desperately and leaned against his side as they shuffled along, the crowd buffeting them. The boy seemed half-asleep on his feet, and the old man wasn't any steadier. Piper grew worried for them, as time and again some abler person jostled them aside. At times Sontag wavered as if he might fall. She looked up at Mitch and saw that he was equally troubled.

"Come on," he said, grabbing her hand and shouldering his way through the crowd, towing her behind him. "Excuse me. Excuse me. Excuse me."

They caught up with the pair about halfway to the

exits. Mitch released Piper's hand to toss Robin up into his arms. The child wrapped himself around Mitch unquestioningly, his head dropping onto Mitch's shoulder. Piper slipped an arm around the old man's bent shoulders—he was no taller than the tip of her nose—and did her best to steady him as they inched toward the lobby.

The crowd scattered in all directions once they made it through the exits, and Sontag paused for a moment to recoup his strength and get his bearings. He glanced at Mitch and his dozing grandchild. Wincing, he opined, "I can't carry him anymore. He's dead weight when he's exhausted. I shouldn't have agreed to stay past the intermission, but he loves the music so."

"Just show us which way to go, sir," Mitch said mildly.

The elderly man glanced around and pointed. "The car's waiting outside that door." It was almost opposite the door through which they had entered at the beginning of the evening.

"Just follow me," Mitch said, starting across the crowded lobby. People were lined up twenty deep at that particular door, but Mitch wasn't letting that deter him. He once again forged a path, one arm holding Robin snug, the other ushering both Piper and Mr. Sontag.

They reached the sidewalk in far less time than Piper had expected. An African-American driver wearing blue jeans, a white sport shirt and a red ball cap popped out of an aging limo and hurried around to open the rear door before reaching up to take Robin from Mitch.

"Aw, the baby's sleeping," he cooed, dipping under the boy's weight. "It's all right, honey. Red's got you."

"Put him in this side," Sontag instructed the driver. "I'll go around."

"Aunt Velma's got your bed all turned down," Red was telling the grumbling child. "You just rest yourself till I get you home."

While he tucked the boy into the back seat of the limo, clucking like a mother hen, Sontag turned to Mitch and Piper. "Red's my arms and legs. He'll take care of us now. Thank you both for your assistance."

"Our pleasure," Mitch said for both of them.

Piper nodded. "It was nice to meet you."

"We'll see one another again," Sontag assured her, placing his gnarled hands on her shoulders. "Mitchell's too smart not to keep you on his arm." Stretching up, he kissed her cheek lightly with his papery lips before laboriously turning away.

The driver stepped up to take his elbow and ease him down off the curb, chiding gently, "I swear, Ivan, you're gonna worry me to death. I've been waiting for y'all this hour. You're no spring chicken to be staying out all night."

"Stop your scolding, man. It was the boy."

"Uh-huh."

Ignoring that drollery, Sontag looked back over his shoulder. "Take your pretty bird home, Mitchell," he ordered, "and give my best to your parents."

"Yes, sir."

Red settled the old man into the car beside Robin and hurried to get behind the steering wheel. Piper waved as Mitchell guided her away.

They didn't try to go back through the bustling lobby, electing instead to walk around the building,

though that was the longer way. Mitch kept to the
outside next to the curb, his arm protectively circling
her waist. He seemed to be in a hurry, so much so
that they crossed the street against the light, weaving
in and out amongst the cars queued up at the intersection.

He took one look at the mob waiting for the elevators in the parking garage and headed for the stairs,
asking, "Do you mind?"

She shook her head. "It's just one floor."

"Come on, then."

He took the steps two at a time, but didn't try to
rush her as she climbed steadily in her heels. Once
they reached the correct level, however, he set off at
a long stride, requiring her to pace swiftly in order to
keep up.

She bit back a sigh of relief when they reached his
car. He hurried ahead and had the passenger door
open for her when she arrived. She dropped smoothly
into the seat. He was in his place next to her before
she got her safety belt buckled. In an instant the motor
was running, and they were nosing out into the exiting
traffic.

Thankfully it was moving swiftly, but when she
looked over at Mitch, he was rubbing a hand over his
jaw in apparent frustration.

"Are you okay?"

"Hmm?" He smiled at her suddenly and reached
across to squeeze her hand. "I'm great."

The car in front of them swung onto the street, and
Mitch took his hand back in order to follow suit, turning the wheel swiftly to the right and gunning the
engine. They caught two red lights, and then sailed
smoothly through emptying streets. Within a quarter

hour the smart foreign coupe was pulling into one of the exterior parking spaces in front of her building.

She opened her mouth to say that getting out of the garage had been relatively painless after all, but she would have been talking to an empty seat, as he was already out and closing the door. The man was in an almighty rush all of a sudden, she thought, as evidenced by her door popping open and his hand reaching down for her. She had no sooner slung the chain strap of her handbag over her shoulder and set a foot on the ground than he was pulling her up.

He looked down at her, and his hand slid up her arm. A car turned off the street into the tiny lot. Mitch dropped his hand, clamped it around her elbow and ushered her toward the security gate. He was punching in the code before they even came to a stop, and then the gate was swinging open and she felt herself carefully guided through it.

"Your key?" he asked, striding forward. "Where's your key?"

She stumbled slightly when she looked down to open her handbag, but he barely broke stride, drawing her along with him. She managed to get the key out of her little bag by the time they reached her apartment, and Mitch was quick to take it from her fingers. He turned the key in the lock and pushed open the door. She found herself being swept into the darkness, the door closing behind her.

"Mitch…" she began, shocked into silence when he abruptly spun her around.

"At last—an appropriate moment," he said, cupping her face with both hands.

Realizing suddenly just why he was rushing so, she burbled a laugh, but then his lips gently met hers, and laughter turned to delight as his lips drew her in. After a long moment he slowly lifted his head, gradually breaking the kiss.

Her eyelids fluttered up, feeling weighted, as warmth pulsed through her. She found herself looking straight into evening-sky eyes. His thumb lightly rubbed across her lower lip, and then he dropped his hands. Sliding his arms around her, he pulled her close, tucking her head beneath his chin.

For several moments he simply held her, but then he curled a knuckle beneath her chin and tilted her face up again. Once again, his kiss was tender. Cradled against him, she slipped her arms about his waist and let herself be thoroughly kissed. She felt toasty and strangely energized by the time he lifted his head again, just long enough to lay his cheek against hers.

"Well," he commented softly, that one word holding enough meaning to describe all the wonders of the world.

She put her head back and laughed throatily. It was the fullest, most right moment that she had felt in a very long time.

"I should go," he said, smiling broadly. "It's getting late."

She nodded and felt him slip away. "It was a wonderful evening, Mitch. Thank you."

He shook his head and pressed two fingers across her lips. "I'm not the one to thank."

She knew what he meant, and she was surprised by how very much she wanted to believe that this night, even their meeting, had been engineered in heaven.

"Will I see you tomorrow for lunch?"

"Absolutely."

With that he left her alone in the dark.

Piper sighed and leaned over to switch on a lamp before gliding dreamily from the room, humming to herself.

Perhaps she really had done the right thing by coming here. She began to feel a real burgeoning of hope. It was enough to hold the past at bay for a little longer.

Mitch arrived ahead of her at the square on Wednesday, but she showed up with a bright smile for him a few minutes later, bubbling with the discovery that after a year of employment her company would pay her tuition if she went back to college for her master's degree. She would have to continue working, of course, and promise them a year of employment after earning the advanced degree, but it was something to consider. He suggested that it couldn't hurt to investigate the course material and majors offered. She said she'd look into it and asked if he'd write her a recommendation, should one be required.

That seemed to say to Mitch that she was looking toward the future—and that he just might be in the picture.

"Sure, if it'll help, but I'd think one of your managers here or at your old job would carry more weight."

"Could be," she said, ducking her head, suddenly subdued.

"Look," he counseled gently, "I know you're not crazy about your job, but there must be a reason you were led to it. I'm a firm believer that there are no accidents in life."

She looked up at him sharply. "You really think that?"

"Yes."

She bit her lip, and after a moment shook her head, but she said no more on the subject, remarking instead about how much she had enjoyed the previous evening's concert. He wondered what it was that wouldn't let her believe that God was in control of her life when she so obviously wanted to.

On Thursday she told him of Thailand, of her earliest memories there, of being wet so much of the time that her fingers and toes stayed puckered and her mother had to scrape things off her skin. She remembered being ill and taking a boat and then a cart and finally a train to see a doctor. She spoke of her early weeks at boarding school, how strange it was to be surrounded by Caucasian faces and to hear English spoken all the time and how exposed she'd felt sleeping without a mosquito net.

That day he also found himself talking about his own life. He told her about meeting Anne in college. The sweetness of the recollection surprised him, but not so much as the ease of it. Had he feared the pain so badly that he hadn't allowed himself to dwell on the memories? He decided that must be the case when she asked, in the course of conversation, about his wedding to Anne. He found himself describing the event with much the same joy as he had experienced it.

"I thought the whole thing was much ado about nothing," he told her, amused at himself now. "We'd been engaged almost two years. Both sides of the family knew every detail of what was going to take place. I was sick of the whole thing, if you must know, and then that morning it hit me. Bam! 'This is it, buddy. You're about to be a married man, a real grown-up.' I got sick to my stomach.''

"Were you scared?" she asked, oddly prescient.

"Terrified. I couldn't get dressed for throwing up. It was so bad that my best man, my cousin Jack, took a black marker and wrote on the soles of my shoes—new, pale leather, mind you—the words *Help me.*''

"Oh, no.''

Mitch had to chuckle. "Imagine kneeling in front of two hundred and fifty people with the words *Help me* written on the bottoms of your shoes. *Help* on the left, *me* on the right. At the time I couldn't imagine what all the snickering was about.''

"What an awful joke to play,'' she said.

He just grinned. "I know someone else who would agree with you. It was all over, and we were out in the vestibule waiting for the procession to play out in reverse so we could go back and take *more* pictures. Me, I was just relieved to have gotten through the ceremony without fainting—or worse—and there comes my mother. She literally chased Jack, smacking him with her open hand, and him a foot taller than her.''

"I don't blame her,'' Piper muttered, but it all seemed like a lark to Mitch now.

"And Dad—'' Mitch remembered aloud, "He couldn't stop grinning all the time he was telling me about seeing my feet come up as we knelt.'' Mitch shook his head. "When Annie found out, she nearly swallowed her tongue.''

"I would imagine so,'' Piper said, obviously empathizing with Anne's reaction.

"They had to retouch the photos,'' he recalled.

"Well, thank goodness for that."

"We were married a year before I could have Jack over to dinner."

"He'd have had boiled shoe leather at my table," Piper vowed, but she was smiling as she said it.

"When Anne died," Mitch said, surprising himself again, "Jack sobbed like a baby."

Piper made no comment for a moment. Then she softly said, "You loved her very much, didn't you?"

He nodded. "Still do. Always will. But my life didn't end with Anne's." He had never been more keenly aware of that fact than now.

Piper looked down. She always did when she wanted to hide her thoughts, but he waited, and she finally squinted off into the distance, asking, "How do you ever get over that kind of pain?"

For a moment he felt as if the world must be holding its breath. It was the same feeling he sometimes got in a group session when one of the newer members approached a breakthrough, as if the situation might have suddenly become real or a little more manageable or just slightly understandable on some, any, level. He didn't think it was his expectation at work here. She had never said that she had lost someone; she hadn't come to group for counseling. It was just something he sensed in her, an all-too-familiar ache and confusion with which he keenly identified. Was she ready to talk about it finally? Hoping that she was, aware that she might not be, he considered his words carefully.

"Grief is very personal. No two people grieve in the same way. In my case, I don't think I'll ever 'get over' the death of my wife, but I have finally gotten *past* it. And I'm ready for…more."

He wanted to ask her for whom or what she was grieving, but he knew better than to push. When she was ready, she would tell him about it. And maybe he was wrong. He hoped, prayed that he was wrong, because he didn't want grief to be the reason that God had brought them together—not the only reason. He was torn between relief and concern when she abruptly flashed a bright, brittle smile at him and the moment passed.

Leaning into him, she said, "Worked on any interesting cases lately?"

He chuckled. She wasn't even trying to be very subtle about changing the subject. "You could say that. Would you believe two cabbies going at each other with knives because of tribal rivalries they should have left behind them in Africa? The sad thing is that one of them is a doctor who can't practice here until he gets a license, and he can't get a license until he lands a residency, and how is he going to get a residency with a felony conviction?" He shook his head. "Worse, INS may deport him."

"What are you going to do?" she asked, concern evident in her voice.

"Right now I'm trying to prove that deporting him would put him in jeopardy due to the same tribal rivalries that landed him in this mess. If I can swing that, I can plead him down to a misdemeanor on self-defense. In the meantime I've arranged—"

"Counseling," she supplied.

"ESL classes," he corrected, bumping her with his shoulder. "English as a second language."

Her amber eyes glowed warmly. "You're a very nice man, did you know that?"

He wanted to ask if he were nice enough for her

to trust him with whatever was bothering her, but his training won out. Or was it something else? Was the truth more that he was afraid to know her secrets? He searched for her hand with his, and when it came to him, curling into his own, he decided that was enough. For now.

She laid her head on his shoulder, and he couldn't resist dropping a light kiss just below the tiny peak in the center of her hairline.

They would have time to say all that should be said, he told himself. Maybe a lot of time.

Maybe they would even have the rest of their lives.

On Friday Piper was waiting when he got to the bench they had staked out as their own. She smiled up at him, and then as he folded himself down onto the seat next to her, she pursed her lips and leaned forward almost absently. He kissed her, just a light smacking of lips, and wondered if she even realized what she'd done.

"How was your morning?"

"Fine. Yours?"

"Okay."

She was unwrapping a sandwich on her lap. He reached into his coat pockets for the first of two sandwiches and a bag of chips that he had brought for himself.

"What've you got?"

"Chicken salad," she said around a bite. "You?"

"Fried bologna."

"Yuck."

He chuckled. "Guess that means you don't want to trade."

"You guess right," she said from the corner of her

mouth. Then she swallowed, looked at him and said, "You want to come swimming on Saturday?"

"*Swimming?*"

"The pool at the apartment is heated, but they're not stupid enough to keep it going all year round. It closes after this weekend, hence the building-wide pool party."

"Ah." He was smiling inside. "Sure, I'd like to come."

"Okay. About two? There's going to be a big cookout later in the afternoon. Melissa and I bought burger makings last night."

"Should I bring anything?"

She shrugged. "If you want. Chips, maybe, or soft drinks. I'm making cookies for dessert, and Melissa's doing coleslaw."

"Sounds good."

She lifted a cautionary hand. "Just warning you. They play their music loud."

"No problem. I'm not a partyer, but I'm not a kill-joy, either."

"If it gets rowdy, we'll just go in and watch a movie or something."

"My thought exactly."

They smiled at each other, in complete accord, and he wondered if she knew that he was teetering right on the edge of falling totally in love with her—and whether or not it was what God intended.

Chapter Nine

Mitch actually had to go out and buy a bathing suit, not an easy task in late October even in Texas, where it stayed warm far later than in most of the country. The old one that he habitually wore for swimming at the gym was faded and beginning to come apart at the seams—the result, no doubt, of repeatedly being soaked in chlorine without rinsing. He'd have to remember to bring the new one home occasionally and throw it into the wash.

Once he had the suit on under his jeans and T-shirt and a towel in the car, it was just a matter of picking up a six-pack of canned cola and a large bag of potato chips. On impulse, he snagged a small jar of jalapeños, then on second thought he put it back and took a larger one. He couldn't be the only one who liked a little fire on his burger. Then he found some hot mustard and, well, he couldn't pass that up, now, could he? And, oh, man, he thought, he'd forgotten all about those peppered pickles that his mom used to keep for him! Why hadn't he remembered to buy them before?

"No antacids?" the clerk asked as she checked him out.

"Nah, that's what the cola's for."

He said the same thing to Piper later as she was unpacking the grocery sack he'd hauled into the courtyard of her apartment. She seemed equally unconvinced, but Scott Ninever was "blown away" by the peppered pickles.

"Hey, man, where'd you get these?"

"Off the shelf in the grocery store."

"Yum, can't wait to get my teeth around some of these babies."

"Help yourself."

"Thanks." He promptly put down that jar and reached for the jalapeños. "We can grill these right into the burgers. What d'you say?"

"Sounds good to me."

"O-kay! Man food."

Mitch laughed, because Scott Ninever was little more than a boy. It was shocking to realize that he'd been about the same age when he'd married Anne.

The Ninevers were sweet kids, and they'd clearly taken Piper under their combined wing, but they made Mitch feel as old as the hills. Most of the other apartment residents were young, too, most of them in their mid- to late twenties, about Piper's age. Yet she somehow seemed more mature than they did.

Maybe it was because she didn't pile on the makeup or wear her hair in a wildly spiked or scissored style or put strange piercings in odd places. Piper's beauty was all natural, and it was blatantly obvious, especially in a swimsuit—even a conservative one-piece with a filmy little sarong-type thing covering her from knees to waist.

Other women in the group wore much less, but not one of them affected Mitch like the sight of Piper, with her bright braid hanging down her back. It fell over the crisscrossed straps of her simple moss-green suit. Her feet were bare, and he couldn't stop looking at her little toes with their coral-painted nails. Something about them struck him as highly intriguing. It was almost embarrassing. He tried to keep his gaze on her face, but then her mouth just made him want to kiss her.

Funny, but he missed that little greeting kiss that he'd had only once before. How ridiculous was that? If they hadn't been part of a group, he'd have initiated it himself.

Not many of the dozen or so women in the crowd actually got into the pool, and they didn't parade around in their bathing suits for long, either. Seventy degrees with a breeze was just too cool to walk around with that much exposed skin. Most of them donned clever little cover-ups well before the sun began to hang low in the western sky. Piper did get into the water, but kept her hair dry as best she could, pinning her braid up on top of her head. Mitch kept an eye on her as he played a rowdy game of water polo with the guys. By the time they called it a match—no one had bothered to keep score for longer than a goal or two at a time—she was out and sitting on the deck with Melissa, wearing jeans and a short green cardigan with a hood and long sleeves. Her toes were covered with canvas slip-ons.

Mitch dried off and tugged on his jeans and T-shirt before joining Scott at the grill. The guys were all helping themselves to his jalapeños, pickles and hot mustard. The ladies were concentrating on salads and potato chips. Melissa and Piper split one of the "monster burgers" that the guys had tossed onto the grill. Everyone ate Piper's chocolate chip cookies as if they were going out of style, including him, though he had to practically snatch them out of other people's mouths.

As Piper predicted, the music did get loud around sunset, and Mitch figured it was just a matter of time before some knucklehead tossed one of the women into the pool just to hear her screech. He slipped a warming arm around a shivering Piper and asked if she was ready to go in. To his surprise, Scott invited himself and Melissa along.

"Hey, yeah, let's go in. You guys play any games?"

Mitch looked to Piper, who telegraphed a shrug with her eyebrows. "Sure. What kind of games? Board games? Dominoes?"

"No, man, like video games. I've got a cool one upstairs, for team play, you know?"

Mitch looked to Piper again, saying hesitantly, "I've used a controller a time or two."

"I've got more cookies in my apartment," Piper suggested, pointing toward her door, "but no computer or DVD player."

"I'll grab my stuff," Scott said. "Lissa, help me?"

"Sure thing, babe." She flipped Piper a wave as she turned to follow her husband, saying, "We'll be right down."

Standing close to Piper, Mitch watched them climb the stairs, one thumb snagged in his belt loop. "Looks like we're going to play video games."

"Do you mind?" She seemed concerned.

"Nah. Might be fun."

She let out a little breath of relief and smiled as she turned toward her apartment. He fell in beside her, not at all surprised to hear shrieking and a large splash, accompanied by laughter. Glancing back over his shoulder at the pool, he urged her to pick up the pace.

"Looks like we're cutting out of here just in time."

"It's been fun, though, hasn't it?" She sounded worried again.

Smiling down at her, he said, "I've had a real good time. I always do when I'm with you."

She smiled and dipped her head, a faint blush rising to her cheeks. "I always have a good time with you, too."

"Not always," he said before he thought.

She stopped dead in her tracks, looking up at him. They were both remembering the times she had run away in tears or pulled back in anger. "It was never because of you, Mitch."

"Then why won't you tell me about it?"

Stark pain drained her face of color and sent her gaze slithering away. "Tell you about what?"

"Piper, don't. Honey, can't you see that I'm here to help you?"

"I'm not one of your legal aid clients," she snapped.

"And I'm not speaking to you as an attorney."

"What, then?"

He cupped her face in his hands. "As someone who cares, Piper, someone who cares deeply for you."

He couldn't tell if her expression was one of horror

or fear, but then she burrowed into his arms, pressing her cheek to his chest.

"I care for you, too. Isn't that enough?"

He supposed it would have to be. For now.

"So long as you know that I'm here for you."

"I do. And I'm here for you, too."

To a point, he thought. But not to the point of trust.

Oh, Lord God, have I read this all wrong? Is she for me? Or is it all the other way? If I'm supposed to be helping her somehow, I'm sure not doing a very good job of it. Help me get my personal desires out of the way, so I can know what I'm supposed to be doing!

She pulled back then. "Come on. I think I'll make some hot tea to go with the cookies." She wrinkled her nose. "Do you think Melissa and Scott like hot tea?"

He chuckled and grabbed her hand. "If we can play video games, they can drink hot tea."

"Oh, wait, *you* don't like hot tea."

He just smiled at her. "I must like it more than I realized. It actually sounds pretty good."

She lifted her eyebrows skeptically at that, but then laughed and hurried once more toward her apartment.

Great, he thought, just what I need in my life— another woman whose hot tea I can't refuse.

The thought was not particularly dampening.

Thankfully, Piper's hot tea was not so bad. The peppermint flavoring enhanced the chocolate in the cookies quite nicely, and Mitch decided that he was going to buy his mom a large quantity of the stuff for Christmas. Melissa downed her share, but Scott let his go cold, too caught up in the video game to bother with it. The cookies he could stuff into his mouth in the blink of an eye, between finger maneuvers in the game.

At the mechanics of the game, Mitch wasn't much competition for Scott, but Melissa was, so they teamed up that way, leaving Piper to play with Scott. She gave a pretty good accounting of herself, especially when it came to strategic decisions, which also happened to be Mitch's forte. Before long it became apparent that they were fairly evenly matched as teams. Scott and Piper won in the end, but it was close.

Melissa proposed a guy-gal competition, and she and Piper made a good game of it, though at the last the guys ran away with it. Mitch and Piper tried it together and got soundly whacked by the more experienced husband-and-wife duo.

All in all, it was more fun than Mitch had anticipated, and he spent several minutes just practicing his thumb and finger technique with Scott, who had an intimate working knowledge of the controller and the medium. It was going on ten o'clock when Mitch finally set aside the controller, stretched and said that he ought to be heading home.

Scott instantly rose and began unhooking his DVD player from Piper's TV. Mitch helped Piper gather up the cups and saucers and sweep away the cookie crumbs from the top of the coffee table, intending to stall until the Ninevers had gone, but after stacking the cups in Piper's tiny dishwasher, he returned from the kitchen to find them still standing around the door, their electronic gear in hand.

"Listen, Mitch," Scott said, "how'd you like to hang out at the arboretum with us tomorrow? We go there on Sundays sometimes, me and Lissa and Piper.''

Piper smiled and lifted an eyebrow inquiringly. Mitch tucked his thumbs into his back pockets, considering.

''Tell you what, you three join me at church tomorrow morning, then we'll spend the afternoon at the arboretum together, and lunch will be on me. What do you say?''

Scott shrugged and looked at Melissa, who looked at Piper. Mitch looked at Piper, too, noting her sudden pallor, but then she smiled and nodded, and he wondered if he was imagining it. Maybe she was just tired.

''Okay,'' Melissa said, ''why not?''

Mitch grinned. ''Great! There are two morning services. We can do the later one. Why don't I drop by about ten-fifteen and pick up everybody? Won't have to bother with directions then.''

''Is it far?'' Melissa asked.

''Quite close, actually—mile, mile and a half, maybe.''

''So do I, like, have to wear a suit?'' Scott wanted to know.

Mitch shook his head, trying not to smile. ''The late service is the contemporary one. All the suits will be at the first. Well, nearly all.''

''Cool.''

Mitch brought his hands together in front of him. ''Okay. So I'll see you tomorrow.''

Scott took the hint and finally headed out the door.

''We'll come down in the morning, Piper. Be here before Mitch,'' Melissa said.

''Sounds good.''

"I don't suppose you've got any more of those cookies for munching at the arboretum?" Scott wanted to know.

Piper laughed. "Sorry. You cleaned me out. I'll bake some more this week."

"Dude, those things are yum," he declared, rubbing his amazingly still flat middle.

"Thanks. Good night."

"Night."

She closed the door behind them and looked at Mitch.

"Dude," he said, mimicking Scott's inflection, and reached for her, and she laughingly came into his arms, locking her hands just above his waistband in the back. He let his own hands slide lightly across her back.

"You were sweet to put up with them all evening," she said.

"No, no. I like them. They're a fun young couple, and they obviously care about you. That's enough for me."

"Mitch," she said, suddenly reticent. She brushed a hand across his shoulder.

"What is it, honey?"

She tilted her head. "I—I don't think they've had much experience with church."

"Not everyone's as blessed as we are."

She shot him a surprised, somewhat troubled look.

"We both have parents who saw to it that we would have lifelong experience with church," he explained.

She smiled then. "You're right."

If her smile lacked its usual luster, well, he told

himself, she was definitely tired. A person could stand only so much fun in a single day.

"I'd better go, let you get some rest."

She nodded and leaned into him, turning her face up, her arms folded between them. He took that as a sign that he should keep it brief, which he did, indulging himself in the sweetness of her lips only for a moment before pulling away and lightly kissing her forehead.

"See you tomorrow."

She nodded and smiled as he went through the door, closing it gently behind him.

The action around the pool had waned somewhat, but a fire had been lit in one of the braziers placed at intervals around the deck. Several people clustered around it as music blared from speakers in the potted trees at each corner of the courtyard. Someone called out a farewell, and Mitch lifted a hand in acknowledgment.

They were a friendly bunch, perfectly nice, and several of them he wouldn't mind knowing better, including the Ninevers. But somehow it felt wrong to be leaving Piper here with them, even if she was tucked safely inside her apartment. He couldn't help noting it had all the warmth and personality of the average hotel room.

He told himself that it was too soon to be feeling so proprietary where she was concerned, but he was hung on the notion that she really ought to be going home with him. He prayed that was more than his own neediness and impatience speaking.

Piper looked up at the tall tan brick building with its steep roof and modernistic spire reminiscent of a ship's long prow and chided herself for the umpteenth time. Honestly, this quivering in the pit of her belly was pure nonsense! How many times in her life had she walked into a strange church?

She couldn't begin to count the number of places to which she had accompanied her father on speaking engagements, let alone those churches she had attended for a simple Sunday service. It was true that in recent years she'd regularly attended the same "home" church in Houston, but she'd still managed to accompany her parents—who kept busy schedules despite their retirement from the mission field—several times a year, as her work had permitted. A new church was nothing "new" to her, for pity's sake, so why this gut-wrenching, heart-palpitating dread?

As if sensing her turmoil, Mitchell slipped an arm about her shoulders, the comforting weight of it jogging up and down as they walked side by side toward the elaborately carved front door. Easily ten feet tall and four inches thick, the heavy portal nonetheless swung effortlessly out as he gently tugged the twisted, wrought-iron handle.

The low, familiar hum of people talking enveloped them as they entered the posh foyer, and almost at once a friendly hand came their way, offered by an official greeter with an "Ask Me Anything" button pinned to the lapel of his sports jacket. Mitch greeted the man by name and made the first of many introductions.

"These are my friends, Piper Wynne and Scott and Melissa Ninever."

"We're glad to have you with us this morning," the fellow said heartily, shaking each hand and repeating the names in turn. Then the thing that Piper dreaded most came about as he turned back to her, the gleam of speculation in his friendly gaze. ''Wynne, that's a mighty familiar name. How do you spell that?''

Before she could answer, Mitch slapped his church brother on the shoulder and said, ''If you're thinking Ransome and Charlotte, you're on the right track.''

''Any relation?''

Piper made an effort to smile rather than cringe. ''They're my parents.''

''Wow!'' the man exclaimed. ''I've read all of your father's books.'' Thankfully, others crowded in behind them just then, and he was forced to let them go.

Piper glanced uneasily at Scott and Melissa and saw the curiosity in their eyes. Sighing inwardly, she allowed Mitch to usher her deeper into the wide, arcing foyer with its dense plum-colored carpet.

''Mitch,'' she whispered, prompting him to bend his head to hers solicitously, ''I'd rather you didn't mention my parents.''

''Oh? Can I ask why, sweetheart?''

Sweetheart? she thought, trying not to be distracted by that casual endearment. ''It's just that it sort of leaves the Ninevers out of it.''

''I'm not sure I follow.''

''I don't want Scott and Melissa thinking I'm more welcome than they are just because of my family.''

''You're right. That wouldn't do. Still, you must realize that ninety percent of the people in this building will make the connection on the strength of your surname alone.''

She sighed. ''I know.''

He gave her a measuring look. Henceforth, however, he made every effort to deflect speculation, even introducing her simply as Piper. Nevertheless, by the end of the service, the news had spread.

A slim, attractive, middle-aged woman bustled up to Piper just as she was stepping into the aisle and gushed, "I attended a women's retreat where your mother was the guest speaker. Such an interesting life you've led! Could we entice you to speak to our women's mission group?"

"Oh, I'm sorry. I leave that sort of thing to my parents," Piper said, very uncomfortable.

"Piper's a nurse," Mitch added helpfully.

"Really?" the woman persisted. "In what mission field?"

"I'm not in mission work. Actually, I'm in managed care right now."

"Ah."

That single syllable contained all the confusion, surprise and, she imagined, disapproval that Piper had come to expect. Why was it, she wondered, that she was presumed to have a calling just because her parents had? Her brother had often fought the same assumption, but then a year after college he had entered seminary. She couldn't help wondering if everything might have been different if he'd resisted the expectations of others.

She shook her head. Gordon was a wonderful pastor, and even now he was plagued by those who continually expected him to surrender to foreign mission work, when it was clearly not what he was meant to do.

"Maybe later, Caroline," Mitch said, and Piper realized that the woman had been speaking, presumably to her.

"I'm sorry. What were you saying?"

"I thought you might want to join our mission group," the woman, Caroline, offered, not unkindly.

"Oh, ah, Mitch is right. I haven't made a decision about a local church yet, but thank you for the invitation. I'll certainly keep it in mind."

The woman looked past Piper to Melissa then. "What about you?"

Melissa glanced at Piper. "I'm not even sure what a mission group is."

To her credit, the woman whom Mitch had called Caroline began a patient and thorough explanation of the group's purpose. Melissa shot a look of surprised interest at Scott when Caroline mentioned sending shoes and Christmas presents to underprivileged children in South America, as well as numerous other local projects.

"I, uh, I'll have to think about it," Melissa said, and Piper could tell by her tone that she meant it.

Piper glanced at Mitch, sure that they would be sharing the same pleased speculation about Melissa's interest in the group, only to find Mitch studying her with a faintly troubled expression. She figured she knew what that was about, so she ducked her head and tried not to think that she had disappointed him somehow. Had he expected her to declare a sudden vocation for exotic foreign fields? Or had the notion that she might be headed in that direction only just occurred to him?

The woman named Caroline moved off, and Mitch guided Piper into the aisle, turning toward the foyer. The resemblance between this church sanctuary and the auditorium of the symphony center downtown struck her suddenly. True, the church was built on a smaller scale, but it was every bit as opulent as the Meyerson. She said as much to Mitch, glad for a "safe" subject for discussion. She felt the weight of his hands rest lightly on the tops of her shoulders as they caught up with the exiting crowd, and he connected the dots for her.

"We used the same architect. Several on the symphony board are members here, too, including my mom."

"Ah."

He chuckled. "You thought I was kidding about her hoping she'd get a classical musician out of me, didn't you?"

She put her head back and looked up at him. "I didn't get the sense that she was disappointed in you in any way."

"I'm very blessed," he said, and that he could think so after the way he'd lost his wife seemed harshly significant to Piper. She lifted her head and gulped, aware that her faith couldn't hold a candle to his.

Always the disappointment, she told herself, once more sick at heart.

They picked up sandwiches at a deli that Mitch liked, probably because they piled on the jalapeños and banana peppers as if they were relish, then stopped by the apartment so the girls could change out of their Sunday clothes. Mitch and Scott were content in their chinos and jeans, respectively, and Scott stayed downstairs chatting with Mitch while Melissa ran up to their place. When Piper came back into the living area wearing jeans and a lightweight, V-necked, turquoise-blue sweater, the two men were deep in conversation.

"Man, I never thought of it that way," Scott was saying. He swept a hand through his shaggy hair. "And it's just a matter of accepting that publicly?"

"Or privately," Mitch said, "depending on your personal convictions. For myself, I don't believe a person can privately accept Christ without it becoming public through personal behavior."

Scott nodded thoughtfully at that. "You know, a lot of it's what Melissa and I have always believed, that you're supposed to love your fellow man and do right by him."

"I think that's a God-given impulse, Scott," Mitch told him. "The problem comes when our earthly impulses get in the way of our godly ones."

"And that's what repentance is about," Scott murmured.

Mitch let that notion simmer in silence for a moment before he turned to Piper. "Wow, that color's really good on you."

"Thanks."

"Ready to go?"

"When everyone else is."

Scott was still mulling over his conversation with Mitch. Piper and Mitch exchanged a knowing look. His gentle smile was full of hope. Piper felt her heart swell. Leave it to Mitch to find a way. The Ninevers were her friends, but he was the one who seemed able to reach out to them in the most important matter.

Melissa tapped at the door and stuck her head in. They were off in a moment, piling into Mitch's car with their picnic lunch and a tie-dyed blanket that Melissa had brought. The mood was gay but strangely serene, as if peace had found them all at the same time.

That feeling deepened for Piper as the afternoon wore on. It was something about this place, she decided. It was a true Eden for her, where all the worries of the outside world were held at bay. Later, when Mitch dropped them all off at the apartment house, he suggested that they follow the same plan the next Sunday. The Ninevers endorsed the idea soundly. Piper went away feeling that she might have found a haven for her troubled soul.

Chapter Ten

Piper noticed that many of the trees were ablaze with autumn color. One half-decent freeze would denude the branches entirely. That time couldn't be far off now, she told herself, strolling silently through the arboretum at Mitch's side. They had left the Ninevers all but dozing on the blanket after devouring a massive lunch that Mitch had ordered specially catered for them.

"I'm sorry about this morning," Mitch said suddenly. "When my mother heard, she...well, I told her last Sunday evening, but I guess my explanation about the Ninevers didn't make a lot of sense, after the fact."

Piper sighed. The pastor had actually announced from the pulpit that the congregation had a special guest in their midst. Piper had felt her face burn hot at the mention of her name. A lengthy tribute to her parents had followed. It was just the sort of thing that they would have hated, but she couldn't help a small lurch of pride as their many accomplishments were listed in glowing terms. That had been swiftly followed by a stab of regret so profound that it had taken her breath. Here in the peaceful sanctuary of the arboretum, however, she could be a little more sanguine.

"I suppose it was bound to happen sooner or later," she told Mitch. "Dad would be horrified, though. He really tries to keep the focus where it belongs."

"I can believe that."

"The problem is, they're just what you think they are."

"Giants of faith," he said, and she nodded.

"It must be difficult when your parents are as well-known in ministry as yours are."

Piper shrugged, secretly pleased that he had divined much of the problem. "It's called the 'PK phenom.'"

"PK?"

"Preacher's kids. We're held to a different standard than others."

"I hadn't thought about it before, but I guess that must be so."

"Believe me, it is." She looked down at the well-mulched path they were treading and added unthinkingly, "I can't tell you what that's meant to my brother."

"How so?"

She looked away, unable to speak of it, unable to speak at all for a moment. Finally she managed to say, "The expectations have just weighed far more heavily on him than on me, that's all."

"It's not a lot different for lawyers, when you think about it," Mitch said after a moment. "I mean, everyone assumed that because Dad was in law I would naturally go into it, too."

"Is that why you did?"

"No. I believe I'm called to it. I believe we're all called to something. I think that's probably why you became a nurse."

Piper bit her lip. Another failure, then, if that were true.

"I think I must have got it wrong," she said, trying to make it sound like a joke. "I think I must have been called to something else." Like messing up.

"What makes you say that?"

She shook her head. "Oh, nothing."

"If this is about your job," he began, but she couldn't allow him to pursue that subject much further. She didn't want to get into why she'd left a hands-on practice, a subject she had studiously avoided during their shared lunchtimes during the past week.

"Come on," she said, slipping her arm through his, "it's too beautiful a day to be talking about anything as unimportant as my job." With that she jogged ahead, giving him a tug.

He joined in, and they ran, laughing and tussling, all the way to the fountains at the back of the park, where they plopped down on a rock as big as a bench. Mitch straddled it, and she sat on the end with her back to his chest, his arms looped about her. For some time they sat there listening to the water spill, then they got up to wander along to the giant wind chimes, which they played like two kids, trying to make some recognizable tune with the thick, long tubes hanging from a crossbeam.

Piper let happiness settle over her, aware that it

would be fleeting, but all too glad to soak up what she could for the present. Such was all, it seemed to her, that this life had to offer. It was enough, surely, to sustain her, and yet she was vaguely aware of a certain exhaustion lately.

It was as if she fought demons in her sleep and the demons were slowly winning.

When they finally wandered back to the picnic spot, Scott and Melissa were gone with the blanket.

"Think we should go look for them?" Piper asked, but Mitch didn't see the point.

Piper seemed troubled, though, so he put his arms around her. More and more lately she seemed to be sinking into a funk. One moment she would be laughing and happy, tossing out clever lines with amazing wit and ease, and then a cloud would pass over her eyes and she'd grow quiet and morose. He had the awful feeling that the real Piper, the vibrant, witty, engaging one, was slowly dying, leaving behind a hollow husk. It had to do with her family, he was sure, but he couldn't imagine what had taken place to drive them apart.

"Don't worry," he said lightly. "Scott and Melissa will be around in a bit. It's not like they can or would leave without us, after all."

"True."

They strolled over to a table and chairs on the veranda of the DeGolyer mansion, which functioned as the centerpiece for the park, and settled down to gaze out across White Rock Lake. Mitch tried to get it out of his head that Piper was hiding some terrible secret, running from something traumatic, perhaps. He was beginning to fear that it might be something that could come back to bite them both, something that might keep them apart. All that stuff about the "PK phenom," as she called it, no doubt had merit, but it couldn't be just that bothering her.

How could he lose his heart to her without knowing what she was hiding from? Yet he was in danger of doing that very thing. Maybe it was time to push a little, let her know that running and hiding would only make matters worse in the long term. He searched for the right words and found what he felt was a good opening to a subject that had been on his mind again lately.

He was ashamed to admit that he'd let the issue of the letter fall by the wayside, allowing all his energies and attention to be taken up by the woman at his side. Now he hoped that one might prompt the other to open up a little.

"Listen, Piper, did you by chance get a letter from the airline telling you that someone had found a personal item that they were trying to return to the owner?"

Her brow furrowed as she thought about it. "Yeah. Yeah, I think I did, now that you mention it. Why?"

"Well, that someone is me."

"Oh?"

He nodded. "You remember that day when we bumped into each other on the sidewalk and I asked if you'd lost a piece of paper or if you'd seen anyone else lose something similar?"

"Sure. What about it?"

"It was a letter, a page out of a letter, really, and I'm still trying to find whoever lost it. Or I should be." He hadn't exactly been following up leads lately—not that he had many to follow. Some pretty little copperhead had distracted him completely. He made a mental promise to get back to the search.

"Is it really that important?" she asked.

"I think it could be. See, the person who lost that letter is running from something devastating—the loss of a son, perhaps."

Piper shivered, and he naturally dropped an arm around her, but his mind was taken with the letter again. The eloquent words came back to him, sifting through his memory like an almost forgotten sigh.

"It spoke of pain and crosses to bear, and it begged for this person, whoever it was written to, not to leave."

She quaked against him, and he glanced up, realizing suddenly that the sun had gone behind a cloud. Though it wasn't particularly cold to him, he linked his hands together, trying to warm her within his embrace even as the letter took shape before his mind's eye.

"I recall one phrase especially," he said, and went on to quote from the letter. "'To forget our dear boy would be to rob us of all the delights he brought into our lives.'" That passage still moved him, and he took a deep breath to help clear away the emotion. "It went on to say how he would hate it if his loss tore apart their family. It's heartbreaking, really, because that's what seemed to be happening. The writer begged this other person not to leave." Mitch tried to remember the exact phrasing. "Something like, 'To lose you, too, is surely more than I can bear.'"

Piper suddenly lurched forward, yanking herself from his grasp and bending at the waist. She promptly threw up her lunch, barely making it to the grass.

"Piper! Honey?"

Shocked, he sprang up belatedly and hurried toward her, but she turned and ran. He went after her, appalled that he hadn't realized that the poor girl was sick. It quickly became obvious that she was heading for the rest room in the rear of the building. He let her go, fighting the urge to follow her into the ladies' room just to be sure that she was all right.

"Piper!" he called out. "Baby, are you okay?"

When she didn't answer, he began to pace, wondering what to do. A young mother with a little girl came along a few moments later, and he didn't think twice about approaching her.

"My girlfriend's sick in there. Would you check on her for me? Her name's Piper."

"Piper," the woman repeated, and he inanely heard himself explaining, "For the bird." That didn't seem to make much sense to the woman, but she nodded kindly and went in with her little girl.

After what seemed like an eternity, Piper came out, mopping her face with a paper towel. Her eyes were red and watering, but he threw his arms around her and hugged her tight with relief.

"Sweetheart, you should've told me you were ill."

She put a hand to her abdomen. "Guess something I ate didn't agree with me."

"I'm taking you home," he said, feeling responsible. He'd handpicked the whole meal, after all. He was going to have a word with the caterers, too, but maybe it wasn't their fault. He'd never had any trouble before with anything they'd provided for him, and he didn't feel sick in the slightest himself—unless he counted the fist inside his chest that seemed to have a death grip on his heart.

Piper was shaking her head. "No, we can't do

that,'' she argued, sounding tired. "Not without Melissa and Scott. Would you just go find them first, please? I'll wait right here." She pointed to a nearby bench. When he hesitated she added, "Please, Mitch."

"Okay, baby, if that's what you want." He walked her over to the bench and sat her down before warning her, "But if I don't find them within the next ten minutes then they'll just have to wait until I can come back for them. Understand?"

"The sooner you find them the sooner we can go," she answered ambiguously.

He set his jaw and hurried off, determined that he would have his way in this. He'd humor her for now, but he wasn't taking any chances with her health, period.

Fortunately, he stumbled across the Ninevers within the first five minutes. He hadn't even finished explaining the situation before they were all on their way back to Piper. She was sitting right where he'd left her, gazing morosely into the distance.

"You okay, hon?" Melissa asked anxiously.

"Just an upset stomach," Piper answered with a wan smile.

Mitch swept her up onto her feet. "I can carry you, if you like."

She shook her head. "No, no. I'll be fine."

He dug out his keys and handed them to Scott. "Bring the car around, would you?"

"Sure thing."

Scott took off at a run, but Melissa stayed behind to add her support to Mitch's. Flanking Piper, they coiled their arms around her and walked her gingerly toward the front of the park.

"Take your time," Mitch counseled.

"I'll be fine," she said, and she kept saying it, but something told Mitch that she believed just the opposite. Shaken, he wondered wildly if she had some fatal disease that she was hiding from him, but surely not.

Please, God, he prayed silently. *Oh, heavenly Father, please. You wouldn't do that to me. Not again.* Then he remembered how the letter writer had put it. *To lose you as well is surely more than God can allow.*

It was a sentiment with which Mitch suddenly identified all too well.

Piper was ill, really ill. She realized that she couldn't go to work, and after dragging herself up the stairs to phone her supervisor from Melissa's apartment, she was almost too weak to get back down again.

"Maybe you should see a doctor," Melissa said worriedly, feeling Piper's forehead for signs of a fever. "I promised Mitch that if you weren't better by this morning I'd see to it."

"It's just a stomach thing," Piper insisted, shaking her head in refusal. "Some sort of bug or virus, nothing more."

But what sort of virus produced such tears as she'd been experiencing? Buckets and buckets of them, and she couldn't understand what she was crying about, for pity's sake.

"Stay here and let me take care of you today," Melissa urged, but Piper was determined not to do that.

"No way. You have to go to work." If this was

some sort of weird bacterial infection, she didn't want to expose her friends to it any more than she already had. Besides, instinct told her that whatever the cause of her physical distress, she was better off battling her personal demons in private.

Melissa protested, but Piper held firm, going back downstairs to curl up on her bed in her sweats. Unexpectedly, she fell asleep at once.

The next thing she knew someone was beating on her door. Feeling as lethargic as when she'd lain down, she struggled up and went to glower at whoever it was, but the instant she opened the door, Mitch enveloped her in a worried embrace, a white plastic bag in one hand.

"You're still sick. I knew I shouldn't have left you alone last night. Melissa says you won't go to the doctor."

"It's just a stomach flu of some sort," she argued defensively. "Honestly, I know when I have to see a doctor and when I don't."

Undaunted by her lousy mood, he chucked her under the chin and kissed her forehead. "All right, I won't nag, but I brought you some canned soup and crackers." He set the bag on the little bar separating the kitchen from the living area. "If you feel up to it, try to eat."

Gratitude mingled with misgiving, both moving her closer to the ever-present tears. "Thanks. I'm sure soup and rest will do the trick."

"Just in case," he said, reaching into his jacket pocket, "I want you to keep this with you today." He produced a cell phone—his own, no doubt. "For me," he added quickly. "How can I concentrate if I don't know that you can get help if you need it? You really ought to think about getting a phone in here, by the way.''

She sighed, knowing that she was not going to do that. She knew, too, though, that Mitch wasn't going away until she agreed to take the phone.

"All right, if it'll make you feel better.''

He smiled and folded her close once more. "That's my girl. Now then, I want you to call if you need anything at all, even if you just want to talk. Okay?''

"I'm going back to sleep,'' she told him, closing her eyes to savor his caring and strength for just a moment longer, "but if I feel worse or discover a great need for more crackers, I'll phone.''

He chuckled and released her, moving toward the door. "I'll be checking in. Take care of yourself.''

"Promise.''

"You're sure you'll be all right?''

She rolled her eyes. "If a certain someone will leave and let me get back to bed, I'll be just fine.''

"Going. Going. Gone,'' he teased, slipping through the door and pulling it closed behind him. She hurried to open it again, catching him still on her doorstep.

"Mitch?''

"Yeah?''

"Thanks.''

He adjusted his jacket, tugging at his cuffs. "Any time, sweetheart. Any time at all.''

Smiling, he kissed her cheek, turned and swiftly strode away. Piper closed the door and pressed her forehead to it. He was so wonderful. She didn't deserve a man like that and didn't kid herself for a minute that she could really have a future with him. In which case, she must be a little nuts to punish herself by continuing the relationship. If she had any sense at all, she'd break it off and avoid his company from this moment forward. Obviously she had no more sense now than she'd ever had.

With tears streaming down her face, she spun and hurried back into the bedroom.

For hours she lay weeping, and really she didn't know why. Every time she thought herself cried out, a fresh onslaught would come. When Mitch called just before lunch, she sniffled so much that he worried she was coming down with a cold on top of everything else. She blamed it on the onion she'd begun to chop for the chicken soup that he'd brought her.

"Onion is good for you, you know," she told him with a sniff. "Lots of healing properties."

"Did they teach you that in nursing school?" he teased.

"Don't be ridiculous. They don't teach anything that useful in nursing school."

"Ha! Well, you must be on the mend if you're cooking."

She assured him that was exactly the case and rushed him off the phone. Afterward, determined to get herself in hand, she chopped onion steadily and added it to the chicken soup, making a meal of it with the crackers and some sliced cheese that she had in the refrigerator. With her stomach full, she ran a hot bath and soaked for half an hour before washing and drying her hair and dressing in comfortable jeans and a baggy sweatshirt.

When Mitch called again, she was able to greet him with a clear nose.

"That's more like it," he said, sounding genuinely pleased. "Those onions must've done the trick."

"That or it's just a twenty-four-hour bug," she said.

"Either way, I'm glad you're feeling better."

"Thanks."

"What would you like for dinner?"

She bit her lip, torn between wanting his company and fearing that she would make a fool of herself again, given half a chance. "I—I wouldn't want to expose you to this, Mitch."

"Honey, I've already been exposed, and I feel fine. I have the constitution of a horse, by the way. Now, what do you want for dinner?" She took a deep breath, stalling, but he pushed. "Come on, what sounds good?"

She blurted out the first thing that came to mind. "Pizza."

He burst out laughing. "You *are* feeling better. Pizza it is. What's your preference? Pepperoni? Cheese? Sausage?"

They settled on half pepperoni and half sausage with, of course, jalapeños. She mentioned putting together a salad to go with the pizza, but he wouldn't hear of it.

"If you want salad, I'll bring salad. You're to do nothing but eat after I get there. Understood?"

She reluctantly agreed, feeling exhausted again although she'd done nothing more than dress and speak on the telephone. Once they'd hung up, she turned on the television, attempting to distract herself with other people's problems on a popular daytime talk show, but the plight of a couple who had lost a child in a tragic drowning accident once more reduced her to tears. She turned on the classical music station and lay down with a damp cloth over her eyes.

When Mitch arrived promptly at six, as promised, she was still listening to music and was feeling better.

He lifted a skeptical eyebrow and insisted, "You are *not* well."

"I didn't say I was," she defended, following him to the kitchen, where he deposited the flat cardboard box and a clear plastic container of salad. "I said I was feeling better, and I am."

He turned to face her, frowning doubtfully, and opened his arms. She walked into them and buried her face in the hollow of his shoulder.

"You don't feel feverish," he conceded.

She turned her cheek to his shoulder, feeling better than she had all day. "By tomorrow I'll be fine."

"You aren't planning to go back to work yet, I hope."

She should. She really should, but she wasn't certain that she could. Just the idea of trekking all the way downtown seemed utterly exhausting. Finally she shook her head.

"I'll wait another day."

"Good. Now, let's get some food in you, and see how it settles. Okay?"

She nodded and got down some plates while he went to the refrigerator for soft drinks. He shucked his coat and draped it over the back of a dining chair, but they ate tucked up on the sofa watching the evening news, since he'd done an interview with the local media that day in reference to his taxi-driver case. The result was a short piece playing to the political principles of asylum and the difficulties that his client had faced and would face again if deported. He played up the fact that his client was a physician and a family man. About the other individual arrested he said very little. All in all, Piper was impressed.

"I didn't want to lay it all on the other guy," he explained, "because my client actually drew his blade first. Then today, after the interview, he finally told me why."

"What did he say?" she asked, taking another piece of pizza.

Mitch wiped his hands on a napkin and looked at her. "He claims that this guy is some sort of war criminal, that he watched him kill innocent women and children in his village, including his own elderly mother."

"Wow. Do you believe him?"

"I think I have to. He gave me the names of half a dozen other immigrants around the state who will evidently back him up." He laid a hand on her knee then. "If you're sure you're on the mend, I might try to see a couple of them tomorrow—one in Austin, another in Houston."

"Absolutely," she said, putting down her half-eaten pizza. She told herself that she was relieved, that she could recover her emotional equilibrium without him there babying her. "Go. Honestly. I'll be fine. This is too important to let some minor indisposition of mine get in the way."

"I don't consider any 'indisposition' of yours minor," he said, squeezing her knee gently, "but this is important, and I should be back by seven or so tomorrow evening."

"Don't worry about it. I mean it, Mitch," she told him softly. "Go do your job."

He nodded, smiled and planted a kiss in the center of her forehead before helping himself to more pizza.

Sitting back, he turned his attention to the weather report. She folded her arms and pretended an equal interest in the television screen, both warmed and chilled—warmed by his so obvious regard for her, chilled by the inescapable fear that it could end very badly indeed.

How could a man like Mitch love a woman who had killed someone dear to her?

Chapter Eleven

Mitch pulled a photograph from his breast pocket and slid it across the table to the scarred, dignified man in the chair opposite him. Tall and gaunt with sad black eyes, shiny black skin and hair prematurely gray, he studied the photo with purposeful intensity, finally nodding his head.

"Aye. That is the man. It was a small company of warriors, but they were armed with machetes and automatic guns." He pecked the photo with the nailless tip of one finger. "This man was the leader. They said they were rebels from the neighboring province, but we heard that he had been refused by one of our women." He shook his head mournfully. "Perhaps that is why they killed the women first, why they attacked when the men were in the fields." He uttered a harsh, guttural word, then translated it for Mitch. "Cowards. They ran when the men came. We heard the shooting and screaming from our plots."

The man confirmed that the doctor had been in the village to administer vaccinations, as he had apparently done several times a year since learning in college of their efficacy.

"Maa'tobe was the first of our people to go to school," the man told Mitch proudly before his face contorted in a grimace. "They tied him to a post and shot him in the legs." He drilled two fingertips against the puckered scars in the hollows of his cheeks. "They shot me through the face as they were running away, and he tended me before he set the shattered bones in his own legs."

Mitch gulped. His client was a hero, as was the courageous gentleman sitting opposite him. That made his burden of legal defense both easier and more burdensome. Heroes were always easier to defend, but failure would result in a huge miscarriage of justice. He could not let that happen. Glancing at his watch, he saw that he still had time to make the Austin-to-Houston flight if he hurried.

"You've been very helpful," he told the man, switching off his tape recorder and nodding at the friend whose office he had appropriated for this interview.

"I'll have my secretary type up the deposition," his friend Dan Creighton offered, "and messenger it to you in Dallas."

"Thanks. I'll expect a bill with it."

Creighton shook his blond head. "I'll take care of it."

"You sure?"

"Consider it my contribution to the cause."

Mitch smiled. Since Dan was assistant counsel to the city of Austin, his endorsement would mean a good deal, a fact Mitch had considered when making his arrangements. He couldn't wait to tell Piper how the case was shaping up. He wondered how she was feeling, and concern threatened his triumph. True, she'd seemed almost her usual self when he'd stopped by that morning, but he couldn't help feeling that something was horribly wrong. His father said it was an overreaction on his part born of experience, and Mitch knew that supposition held truth.

Putting away his concern as best as he was able, he shook the hand of his witness, thanking him again for his time and forthrightness.

"You're helping to bring the murderer of your village to justice," he said, and the fellow beamed at him, revealing healthy pink gums and sturdy white teeth—those in front, anyway. All the back ones were missing, no doubt destroyed by the bullet that had passed through his face.

"I'll be in touch," Mitch promised, pocketing the photo and the tiny tape recorder. Snatching up his briefcase, he nodded once more at his friend and swept from the room, all but jogging toward the elevator.

He made the flight to Houston with minutes to spare, long enough to call Piper on the phone he had borrowed from his mother. She sounded well, said that she was doing some reading and admonished him again not to worry about her. He told himself that he wasn't worried really—he just liked to hear her voice, and, of course, he wanted to share his discoveries with her.

She was suitably impressed and moved. "You say all his back teeth are missing? Couldn't something be done? A bridge, dentures, implants?"

Mitch smiled. It would make a suitable reward, but he couldn't broach the subject until after the case was settled; he must avoid the appearance of purchased testimony. Even then the matter would require diplomatic handling for several reasons. Chiefly, Mitch wouldn't for the world trample on the man's dignity by offering unwanted charity.

"I'll look into it," he promised. "Gotta go, honey. If everything works as planned, I'll see you later."

"Would it be good if I had dinner ready for you?"

"No, no. You just take care of yourself. I'll grab something along the way."

"Whatever you say."

He almost said that he loved her. The words floated on his tongue, and they almost tumbled out of his mouth. Only the shock of realizing they were there at all kept them behind his teeth. He mumbled something about the plane being ready for loading and broke the connection.

Putting back his head, he let the commotion of the crowded airport waiting area fade and thought about what he'd almost said to her. He still didn't know what God's purpose was in all of this, but he couldn't deny what he was feeling. His heart swelled with it. Bright and hopeful, it filled him with a warm glow, and yet it carried the bite of pain beneath the joy of it. If he should lose her, too…

Father God, I need to know. I need to know why You've brought her into my life. I need to understand what You want of me where she's concerned. I know Your plan isn't to break my heart, but that's something I can do to myself if I go wrong with her. Please, God. You know I want to be obedient to Your will.

Moments later when the ticket agent called for boarding, Mitch queued up along with everyone else, troubled despite his earnest prayers. His turn came, and he showed his boarding pass, edging through the turnstile to the enclosed ramp. Two women had passed through in front of him, both carrying brief-cases, and as he followed them up the short, straight, movable hallway he saw something flutter to the floor.

"Ma'am," he called, bending to swoop up the business card as the pair stopped and turned. "You dropped this."

The younger, more smartly dressed of the two smiled and reached out her hand. "Thank you."

Suddenly struck by the thought of the letter that he had found in just such a manner in another airport, he knew he *had* to find its owner. Only then would his prayers be fully answered. A throat cleared, and Mitch realized that he was standing in the middle of the narrow ramp, the women having gone on ahead, as of course they should have. With an apologetic glance at his fellow travelers stacking up behind him, he hurried toward the plane, his mind whirring with plans.

Mitch's second interview of the day followed closely the pattern of the first. If this fellow was more embittered than the other, Mitch deemed it under-standable, given that he had no use at all of his right arm.

"One hand," he said, shaking his left. "One hand with which to feed my family. That is what those bad men did to me. I work in a bakery. Takes me twice as long as anyone else to make the little cakes for frying." He took a deep breath, calming himself, and added, "In America there is no tribe, no village, but at least there is work. Maa'tobe, he saved the arm, but it is useless.'' His brow suddenly furrowed with worry. "You will not tell the Immigration, will you? I refused to answer when they asked me if I could work. Maa'tobe, he told them that I could.''

Mitch felt sure that Immigration was fully aware of this man's physical condition. How Maa'tobe had talked them into letting the fellow into the country anyway he didn't know, but it was one more mark in his client's favor.

"Immigration only cares that you are employed," Mitch assured the man.

The fellow nodded and told his story with clarity and brevity, confirming all that Mitch had already been told. He barely glanced at the photo of Maa'tobe's nemesis before curling his lip in disgust.

"That is the one. If I ever see him in person, I'll stick him with a knife!''

"That's just what's got Maa'tobe in trouble," Mitch told the fellow wryly. "But you're going to help get him out of it. Okay?''

"Okay, sure. But not because he's the chief's son. Because he told the Immigration I could work."

The chief's son. Well, well. Wouldn't Piper find that interesting!

He willfully put aside thoughts of Piper before they could tempt him to forget pursuing another contact in Houston, one he hadn't planned on but should have. He had allowed himself to be distracted too long from his mission of reuniting the lost letter with its troubled owner.

Turning his attention back to the interview, he made short work of it. His own secretary would transcribe the tape, but to expedite the process he took signed affidavits from the two attorneys and one clerk who sat in on the deposition. Then he checked his watch and found a quiet place in a corridor to use the telephone.

Determined in his quest, he'd switched his flight to a later one before he'd left the Houston airport for the interview. Now he dug out the telephone number of one of the airline passengers whose name he'd been given weeks earlier. It was a business number, and several minutes of persuasion were required before he finally talked his way through to the man himself. Once he'd explained his purpose, he was rewarded, finally, with the information he'd been seeking since he'd first spied that folded sheet of paper on the airport boarding ramp more than two months ago.

"Yeah, now that you mention it," the voice on the other end of the telephone said, "I did see her drop a piece of paper. It was one of those old-fashioned kinds that you tear off a stationery pad. You know, the sort with light blue lines on it, personal letter size. I didn't even know they still made that stuff."

"Her?" Mitch prompted, his heart suddenly pounding in his ears.

"Yeah, the little blonde—or redhead. I guess you call her a strawberry blonde, but to me it was more, I don't know, polished copper, maybe. Almost garish, if you ask me, but it looked natural."

"Polished copper," Mitch echoed, the words nearly choking him. It had to be Piper. It had to be, and yet he couldn't quite accept that it was. "Did she wear her hair braided?" he choked out.

"Yeah, that's right. She had a thick braid hanging down her back."

Mitch couldn't seem to get his breath. "You're sure?"

"Yeah, I'm sure." The voice sounded slightly offended now. "I tried to tell her, you know, that she'd dropped something, but she just looked at me, right through me, to be precise. You get how they are, the good-looking ones. Snotty, like every guy's trying to pick them up." He snorted, and Mitch gritted his teeth. It wasn't because of the insult, which barely registered.

Surely no other woman on that airplane, maybe in the world, could fit that description but Piper.

Gut roiling, he thanked the fellow for the information, trying not to think how unwelcome it was, and got off the phone. Rubbing a hand over his face, he let the awful truth sink in. It couldn't be anyone else. That letter belonged to Piper Wynne. Gasping, he tried to wrap his mind around the implications.

She was hiding something—now he was sure of it.

The secret she was protecting, the grief he sensed in her—who had she lost? A child? A son?

Mitch clapped a hand over his heart. *Oh, God, please don't let it be that.*

But if it was, then Piper had a much worse secret than one of loss.

He closed his eyes. If she was married…if she was married… He couldn't even complete the thought.

For long moments he tried not to think at all, but he didn't have to study the problem to know what he had to do next. Whatever the truth was, he had to know it. Only then would he understand how to proceed.

He bowed his head and poured out his heart, needing courage and strength for what lay ahead. Then finally he took out his cell phone again and dialed local information.

"I need a telephone number for Ransome Wynne."

He was late, so late—over three hours—that she was quite convinced he wasn't coming. Obviously something had not gone according to plan, but only the fact that he hadn't called to explain bothered her. She wasn't exactly worried, though it did seem uncharacteristic of Mitch not to keep in touch, so much so that she'd given in earlier and called the mobile number that he'd left her. When she'd heard his mother's voice on the recorded greeting, however, she'd hung up without leaving a message.

She considered and rejected, due to the late hour, calling his parents' house. Surely, at the very least, she would see Mitch tomorrow in the square for lunch. Unable to justify taking another day off, she was determined to go in to work. Perhaps she should call his office and leave a message to that effect. Or perhaps he would call at some atrocious hour, and she could tell him then.

Yes, she decided, he would call in the middle of the night, exhausted and apologetic and full of news about the case—his most interesting to date, as far as she was concerned. And she would be appallingly glad, only too willing to rouse herself from a fitful sleep in order to hear about his day.

Preparing for bed, she brushed her teeth, washed her face and coiled her hair, pinning it up on top of her head so that she could sleep comfortably without rolling over and yanking herself awake every hour or so. She had just kicked off her shoes and pulled her

T-shirt over her head when she heard a tapping at her door; elation shot through her.

The misery that had swamped her these past two days evaporated like so much smoke. Mitch was home! She slipped the T-shirt back on and hurried into the living room in stocking feet, a smile blossoming on her face.

"You didn't have to come by this late," she said, opening the door, "but I'm glad you did."

He stood for a moment, shoulders hunched against the chill night, and regarded her from beneath the crag of his brow. Not the greeting she had expected. A tiny alarm bell sounded in the deepest recesses of her mind. Finally he stepped over the threshold.

He rubbed a hand over his face, palm rasping against the dark shadow of his unshaven jaw. "I brought you something."

A gift? she wondered. More likely a remedy.

"I feel fine," she told him. "I've already laid out my work clothes for tomorrow, so your only concern for tonight should be yourself." She touched a hand to his face. "You look tired."

He nodded and reached into his pocket, extracting a folded sheet of paper. "But you need this, Piper, and I need to talk to you about it. Why didn't you tell me?"

"Tell you what?" she asked, gingerly taking the paper from him. She glanced at it, saw the looping black lines of script and felt horror wash over her. "I don't understand. Where did you get this?"

He simply regarded her, slowly tilting his head to one side. "You don't remember dropping it?"

She couldn't think what he meant, didn't want to

imagine how he might have come into possession of this. She shivered. He knew.

"You really don't remember dropping it," he concluded on a sigh. "I can't imagine how that can be, but you obviously don't. This is the letter that I found in the airport just before I boarded the plane in Houston on the day we met. It belongs to you."

She shook her head. He knew!

"Look at it again."

Mechanically she unfolded the letter and briefly scanned the top few lines.

"...of him will surely never subside," it began, "and will one day be, not a cross to bear, but a cherished joy. His memory will sustain us until—"

She refolded the letter with trembling hands. This was it, then. "You know."

"Of course I know!" Mitch snapped, suddenly angry. "It's part of the letter that your brother, Gordon, pinned to your front door the day before you ran away!"

She wrapped her arms around herself, as if that could keep her from spinning apart. She'd found the letter as she was leaving the house for the final time that last morning, and she'd stuck it into her handbag, unopened. Later, waiting at the airport gate, she'd gone so far as to slit the seal and remove the pages from the envelope, but she hadn't been able to force her eyes past the salutation.

"I never read that letter," she whispered, one more condemning fact in a long list of them.

All the anger seemed to drain out of Mitch. "Oh, Piper," he said.

She couldn't believe that this was happening to her. This ridiculous *accident* was going to cost her everything, all that was left. But then, she'd always known that something would.

"You've obviously read this," she said, waving the letter at him. She was aware that her tone was faintly accusing and that it was unfair, but she couldn't help herself.

"Yes."

"All this interest, all this effort—airlines sending out notices to planeloads of passengers!—for a single page of an unread letter!"

Mitch looked stricken, and for the first time that evening he reached out to her. "Piper, I believe that my finding that letter was no accident. I can help you if you'll let me."

"No one can help me."

"Darling, that's not true. No one blames you for what happened."

She flinched away from him, feeling the words like blows. He knew. He knew. He knew everything, all of it.

As if to confirm that horrible suspicion, he said gently, "I've spoken with your family. They're gravely concerned, and they miss you. Gordon and Jeanette and Thai especially send their—"

Piper clapped her hands over her ears, but her nephew's voice screeched at her all the same. *You killed Asia! We brought him here to you, and you killed him! You killed my brother!*

Hands closed around her wrists. Strong, warm. They tugged gently but firmly, insisting that she uncover her ears, that she hear.

"Asia was coming to you because he trusted you, because you were always there for him."

You know what it's like being a preacher's kid.

*Dad does, too, sure, but he's Dad. You're Aunt Pip.
I can talk to you.*

Piper wrenched free. "Leave me alone!" Corded
arms enveloped her, held her close. She had never
been so terrified of anything, anyone. "Leave me
alone," she sobbed. "Oh, please. Oh, *please,* just go
away!"

"I can't do that."

"Please! Please!"

How could he do this to her? How could he make
her remember? Hadn't she always known, deep down,
that he would do this to her? She tried to get control
of herself, to speak reasonably, to behave reasonably.
She pushed away from him, gulped down the panic,
the horror, took a breath. It was over. Might as well
face it, deal with it. Forget the other.

"Leave now. I need to be alone. I want you to
leave me alone."

He gently smoothed the hair from her face. When
had it tumbled down? "I love you too much to leave
you now."

Love her? That wasn't possible.

Was it?

Something like hope kindled and was quickly
snuffed out again.

How could he love her? How could he love someone who had killed someone else, a person she loved,
a boy who thought she could do no wrong?

Oh, God. Oh, God.

She thought she might simply explode into tiny
fragments too small to be put back together again
even by the hand of God.

Blasphemy, she thought.

Another reason she couldn't be forgiven.

Straightening, she leveled and squared her shoulders, lifted her chin and reached deep inside for the outward calm that had served her so well in moments of crisis. He would not go, she thought, until he had said what he needed to say. People needed to say things when someone died. They needed to comfort, to pretend that life could go on as before. If only she could believe that! Steeling herself, she tucked the letter into a pocket of her jeans and turned to lead him into the living area.

They sat down on the sofa. She perched there, prim and proper, her hands folded serenely in her lap. He sat next to her, his big body slightly angled toward hers.

"I've had a lot of experience with this type of thing, Piper," he began.

"Yes." She nodded solemnly, sure it was true, but of course she couldn't think about that. She had to hold herself together. That was the important thing just now.

"Grief manifests itself in as many ways as there are people to grieve."

Another nod, though she couldn't really hear what he was saying—only the sounds, not the words themselves.

"Guilt is very often a part of it."

"Mmm." A little vocalization kept the repeated nods from seeming mechanical.

"Sweetheart, you are not to blame."

She took a deep breath, holding on by the skin of her teeth.

"Sometimes people blame God," he went on, "and sometimes people, especially people of great faith, blame themselves. Their faith won't let them accuse God or others, you see, so they only have themselves to blame.''

He seemed to think that she was someone like that, someone of great faith. The idea was so ludicrous that she almost laughed. Instead she schooled her face into a solemn, pensive expression.

''Yes,'' she said. ''I see. Well.'' She tried to think of something else to say, something prescient and clever. All she came up with was ''I would appreciate it if you would leave now.''

''Piper.''

''I would really like you to go now,'' she said again, hoping that she did not sound as desperate as she felt. She couldn't look at him anymore, couldn't pretend anymore. ''I need time to think about everything you've said.''

Whatever that was.

He sat there for a long moment. Finally he rose reluctantly. Surging to her feet, she rushed eagerly to the door.

''Piper, please,'' he said, spreading his hands. ''I don't want to leave you like this.''

''No, it's best,'' she replied glibly. ''We both need to rest. Work tomorrow.'' She smiled, holding on for dear life.

One more moment, she told herself. Keep it together for just one more moment.

At the very instant when it seemed that her control would break and the world would come tumbling down on top of her, he walked through her door. She closed it without another word, shot the bolt for good measure and moved swiftly into the bedroom. She closed that door, too, trembling now, quaking in every muscle, agony pouring over and through her. Memories that could no longer be held at bay rushed at her, driving her to the floor. To her knees.

To hell, a hell entirely of her own making.

Chapter Twelve

Rain poured in wind-driven gusts against the night-blackened window behind the rattan sofa where she sat curled against brightly flowered cushions. Safe and snug in her little house, she thumbed through a magazine, sipping peppermint tea gone tepid, despite the sultry temperature.

When the telephone rang she knew immediately, given the weather conditions, that she was being summoned back to work. As one of the few single nurses permanently staffing the city's busiest emergency room, her name was often at the top of the call list when one of her colleagues could not cover his or her shift or catastrophe unexpectedly increased the workload.

Sighing, she set aside the teacup and laid the magazine next to it on the small, round, glass-topped table that her parents had carried all the way from Thailand. Inlaid with delicately carved nacre, it had been given to them on the day of her birth and so had come to her upon their retirement. As the phone bleated again, she reached for it at her side.

Ten minutes later she was backing her economy coupe out of the garage, reflecting that the weather would undoubtedly barrage the E.R. with the victims of auto accidents, one of Houston's most prolific killers. While the thought was depressing, it did nothing to dim her enthusiasm for her work, which she considered vital and challenging. It did, however, encourage her to drive carefully through the rain-washed streets.

Within half an hour of the call she was turning into the hospital employee parking lot, and half a minute later was crossing the street, her ID pass card ready. The familiar wail of sirens told her that she was in for a busy shift.

Just inside the door she met one of her favorite orderlies stacking a cart with clean linens.

"Hello, Gene," she said, swiping her card through the wall-mounted time clock.

"You back already?"

"Yep." She headed down the broad hallway. "Busy night?"

"I'll say! They've called in all the docs."

"Wow."

She smacked a button on the wall and double metal doors swept open just as she reached them. Striding into the triage center, she slid the strap of her satchel from her shoulder and turned a sharp left into the nurses' lounge, momentarily escaping the controlled chaos of multiple desks and glassed-in nursing stations. Lindy, a married friend and co-worker, walked in right behind her.

"Fancy meeting you here," Piper said. "Again, and so soon."

"School bus full of football players," Lindy replied grimly. "I've already heard about two casualties."

"Oh, no."

Quickly Piper threw aside her personal materials, draped a stethoscope around her neck and went out to her station.

"Number two," the shift leader informed her. "Humpty Dumpty coming in now."

Humpty Dumpty was lingo for any sort of injury resulting from a fall. Piper swept back the privacy curtain cordoning off the glassed-in treatment cell from the general area just as a gurney burst through several sets of swinging metal doors. It was immediately followed by two more and a shouting emergency medical technician.

"Burn vics!"

"Burn victims!" the triage station manager exclaimed. "They go to Fourteen."

"Unit Fourteen's full," came the reply. "Dropped two with compounds there myself."

"Crash and burn," said his partner with a tsk.

Meanwhile, the Humpty Dumpty had been wheeled into Piper's "cube." She caught a troubling hack and gurgle as she snapped on a pair of latex gloves and reached to help the technician "off-load"—slide the patient, a young man who was back-boarded and collared, from the gurney to the bed. Mentally cataloging extensive craniofacial damage, she popped her earpieces into place and slid the bell of her stethoscope to the base of the patient's throat just above the collarbone beneath the stabilizing neck brace.

"He's choking. Should've tubed him before you collared."

"Didn't dare," replied the EMT, taking time to slap on sensors and set monitors. "I'm surprised he made it this far. Took impact on his face and throat."

That much was obvious, but a more detailed assessment of the gross facial contusions would have to wait.

"If his windpipe isn't opened, he won't make it any further," Piper concluded, hitting the surgery call button on the wall. A triage nurse in surgery answered at once.

"I need a trache here," Piper shouted into the speaker on the wall.

"Everybody's already on the floor," came the reply. "I'll send Blalock."

Blalock was their most experienced med/surg nurse, but he was no more qualified to perform a basic tracheotomy than Piper herself. It was painfully obvious from the gurgling that he wasn't going to make it in time to help this patient.

Pulling a tracheotomy tray from the supply cabinet recessed into one wall, Piper made a split-second decision.

"Prepare the field," she instructed the LVN who rushed into the space to assist. "I'm going to trache him myself."

"Oh, man," said the EMT anxiously.

"What are you hanging around for?" Piper demanded as the LVN started preparing the field.

The technician shifted from one foot to another. "I promised his family I'd speak to them before I pulled out."

From the tone of his voice Piper knew that he

didn't expect to give them good news, but she couldn't let that deter her. Scalpel in hand, she instructed the assisting LVN, "Break his collar."

The capable older woman with whom Piper had often worked carefully but swiftly released the fastening on the stabilization collar around the patient's neck. Instantly the patient convulsed, gargled and collapsed. The monitors started screaming.

"Crash cart!" Piper yelled, making the necessary incision at the base of the throat and into the esophagus. She inserted the small breathing tube cleanly and smoothly. Blalock swept into the room and without a word produced a breathing bag to attach to the end of the tube. He began to squeeze air into the victim's lungs as the LVN shoved up a torn and soiled T-shirt and squirted liquid on the victim's chest.

He was just a kid, Piper noted dispassionately. She had yet to do more than a cursory assessment of his injuries. Getting his heart started again was more important.

A doctor finally sailed into the room just in time to apply the paddles to the young man's chest.

"Clear!"

The apparatus buzzed. The patient convulsed. The heart monitor continued to squeal out a warning.

The physician yelled, "Charge!"

Piper fell into the familiar routine, applying chest compressions while the machine recharged, then standing back while the doctor applied the paddles. The poor boy's thin chest was reddened and splotchy by the time the doctor gave up several long, frantic minutes later.

What a way to begin a shift, Piper thought sadly.

"Man, that's too bad," the technician said from the

corner where he'd stationed himself during the crisis. "Wish I hadn't told his family I'd speak with them, but I can't say no to a minister."

"Minister?" Piper echoed, hoping it wasn't someone she knew. The doctor thrust a chart at her, having made the necessary notations and signed them.

"He was probably dead when you popped that collar," he commented cryptically before sweeping from the room.

She barely registered the words, as they were not accompanied by a reprimand. Her gaze scanned across the form for a name, curiosity warring with defeat.

Wynne.

The clipboard clattered to the floor. Her gaze flew instinctively to the battered face of the body upon the bed. Could it be? It had to be! She hadn't even recognized him! Reeling backward through the curtain, she stumbled blindly. Her hand found the edge of the desk counter.

"Oh, God, no! Asia!"

Hands grasped at her. Voices spoke her name, but she spun away, running. She didn't even know where she was going until she was in the waiting lounge.

Some innate radar honed in almost instantly on her family now disappearing into a private consultation room where only bad news was delivered. The doctor was there, along with the EMT, who had his cap in his hand as he held the door for her mother. Funny, she couldn't remember his name, though she'd known him for months.

She heard him saying, "I was afraid to remove his neck brace," and she remembered what the doctor had said.

Dead when you popped that collar.

"I did it."

Everyone turned to look at her: brother, father, nephew, sister-in-law. A heartbeat later her mother's head appeared in the doorway. They were weeping, especially her fourteen-year-old nephew Thai. Her father, she noted, had one arm around Gordon and the other around his sobbing grandson.

"I did it," she repeated stiltedly. "It was me. I opened the neck brace, and he died." She still couldn't believe it. That was Asia on that gurney!

Thai began to wail.

"I thought he was choking," she said to herself. "His mouth was torn—I didn't want to go in that way." So she had opened his collar, and he had convulsed. She swayed on her feet, saying again, "I did it."

"You killed Asia!" Thai erupted. "We brought him here to you, and you killed him! You killed my brother!"

Gordon grabbed him—his only son now—with both arms, shushing him as if he were still a babe in diapers.

Piper sat down hard, only vaguely aware that there was no chair in the immediate vicinity.

Asia was dead, and Thai was right. She had almost certainly killed her beloved nephew.

Piper rolled into a tight ball, arms clasped about her knees, and keened. She had weathered those first awful minutes, hours, days, with a dullness born of shock, moving by rote through the hateful obligations of living and mourning. She remembered little of what was said in those next minutes and hours after she'd realized what she'd done, but what she could recall came to her with vivid clarity: the whispered drone of others speaking, Gordon and Jeanette holding on to each other, silent and still, the shadows that lay across the blue tweed carpet in the darkened room.

Most of all, she remembered the way Thai huddled in a chair in a dim corner, bent double, his face in his hands, which were in turn braced upon his knees. Her mother sat with him, looking years older than the last time Piper had seen her. Had it only been days? Her strong, calm, courageous mother looked defeated, beaten, even as she struggled to comfort her only remaining grandson.

It was odd what Piper remembered. She recalled being shocked at the thinness of her father's faded hair as he bowed his head, hair that had once been as lush and vibrant as her own. The room had been cold, so cold that her teeth had chattered. She could still see the strained faces of her co-workers and friends as they filed past her chair, and she remembered especially the way the supervisor of nurses had squeezed her hand, as if they had enjoyed some friendship of which Piper had been unaware, anything other than a distant familiarity and a tenuous sharing of tragedy.

What haunted her most, however, were the eyes of everyone in a position to know what had happened that day. In every gaze of every person who had been there that evening, including her family, she saw the truth, the knowledge, the understanding that she had made the choice that had killed her nephew.

Removing the protective collar from around his neck had allowed the shattered bones of his skull and spine to break apart when he had convulsed. One bone splinter had punctured his battered brain. Piper knew because she had insisted on reading the coroner's report, at least as much of it as she'd been able to bear. Oh, there was no proof that it had happened after she had removed the collar, but she knew that if she had left the collar in place and inserted the tube through his mouth he might have lived. That he might have been paralyzed was of no consequence. He could have survived that. Her family could have survived that. *She* could have survived that.

She had kept herself together only by keeping her distance. Of course, she'd been with the family as often as was expected and proper, but even then she stayed to herself, quiet, hoping they wouldn't notice that she was there any more than they noticed the chairs upon which they sat and the food that kept appearing and disappearing in the kitchen, along with the many whispering faces. Members of her brother's church, friends and family of her sister-in-law, admirers of her parents, even people whom she knew, all swam across her field of vision, mouthing familiar words, bestowing tentative touches, both pitying and accusing her with their eyes. She had nodded and murmured and answered squeeze for squeeze, pat for pat, tolerating the torture because it was her due. She deserved it.

Asia was dead, fallen somehow from his own second-story bedroom window and killed by her arrogance and indifference. She hadn't even known it was him until it was too late. Clearly she did not deserve the family or the life that she'd had. She could never be a real nurse again, never trust herself to make decisions about someone else's medical care. She didn't even have any business reviewing cases on paper. She saw that now.

She'd run all the way to Dallas, sold, given away or abandoned everything she owned, including her house and her car, taken a job about which she knew nothing and cared even less, eschewed a telephone and even the most routine contact with those she loved in an attempt to escape the punishment that she deserved. She hadn't thought it possible to loathe herself more than she already had, but she was wrong about that as she was wrong about so much else.

She couldn't even ask God to help her, to spare her the pain of having killed Asia. Asia wasn't just her nephew; he was her confidant, her buddy, her friend. Mitch had said that he was coming to her because he knew she would help, but she had killed him instead, blindly, arrogantly, in the time it took to snap her fingers.

She couldn't help wondering if there had been others. Certainly others had died in her care. Had she somehow been at fault there, too? She scoured her memory for instances when she might have been, but in the end conclusions were elusive.

What did it matter anyway? She had quite enough guilt to last her a lifetime. A long and lonely lifetime, which was nothing less than she deserved.

Mitch wasn't really surprised when she didn't come to the square for lunch the next day, especially since all he'd gotten whenever he'd tried to call on the phone was his own voice telling him to leave a message, none of which she'd responded to. He did expect that she'd answer her door that evening, so he wasn't sure what to think when that didn't happen.

The lights were on inside her apartment, but it was impossible to tell if she was home or not. He suspected that she was, but if so the portents were ominous.

He tried talking to her through the door. "Piper, it's me. I'm worried about you. Could you open up?"

She made no reply, so he tried again.

"Please, honey. We can work through this if you'll just give us a chance. Please."

He wasn't in the least surprised when that got him no response, and he was hoping against hope, really, that she wasn't there. Maybe the Ninevers would know if she'd gone out, or maybe she was even with them. Praying that he'd find her laughing at one of their off-the-wall remarks, he turned, skirted the pool and climbed the stairs.

Scott answered his knock. Without a word of greeting for Mitch, he called for his wife. A heartbeat later Melissa slid into view wearing a long, tie-dyed skirt with gores of solid colors, cowboy boots and a man's wine-red cardigan over a white T-shirt. Scott slipped an arm around her waist as if expecting that she would need his support.

"Do you know where Piper is?" Mitch asked her urgently.

She shook her head, eyes wide and sad. "All I know is that something's wrong, and she won't talk to me about it."

Mitch sighed. Not good news, not good at all. He warred briefly with the ethical implications of telling what he knew, and decided that divulging only general information was the best course.

"Not long ago someone close to Piper died in tragic circumstances, and she doesn't seem to be coping with the loss very well. I pressed her on it when I shouldn't have, and now she's withdrawn. I'm worried about her, frankly.'' He bracketed his temples with the thumb and little finger of one hand, muttering to himself, ''I shouldn't have left her alone. I shouldn't have confronted her with the letter.''

''What letter?'' Melissa wanted to know, but Mitch just shook his head.

''Doesn't matter. All that matters is that I find a way to make her understand that what she's going through is a natural part of the grieving process.''

''Good luck,'' Melissa said, reaching into a pocket of her voluminous skirt. She pulled out his cell phone and handed it him. ''Piper brought this up this afternoon and said you'd be by for it eventually. She said to tell you that you should forget about her.''

Mitch closed his eyes, the tiny phone heavy in his palm. ''Not much chance of that,'' he whispered.

Scott cleared his throat. ''What're you going to do?''

Mitch took a deep breath. ''I don't know. Pray until I find the answers.''

''Can we do anything to help?'' Melissa asked.

''Talk to her, even if she won't talk to you. Tell her that I'm not going away, that I'm not giving up on her, that God has a plan in all this.''

''That's it?''

''Your prayers would be appreciated, too.''

Scott looked at Melissa, and as one they stepped back, leaving a clear pathway into their home for Mitch. ''Maybe you'd better come in and show us how it's done,'' Scott said.

Mitch didn't know what else to do. He'd tried everything he could think of, even sending a policeman to her door. Once she'd told the officer that she was all right, however, the authorities were powerless to do anything more. The Ninevers had proven a godsend, their burgeoning faith a real blessing in this time of fear, but Piper had forbidden Melissa to talk about him to her. That stung, but Mitch wasn't about to back off now.

Although he'd already failed once at reaching her through her office, he really felt that he had no other choice but to try again, and this time he would not be fobbed off by a simple refusal. He was prepared to make a scene if he had to, even to threaten lawsuits, though that kind of heavy-handedness could easily rebound, since the company was entirely within its rights to deny him access to its employees.

After making that intimidating elevator ride for a second time, he stood for a moment sizing up the staff. The young man had sent him packing before, so Mitch saw no point in trying his luck there again. The older woman looked hard as nails. That just left the younger female. Mitch strode up to the imposing reception desk and slapped a card on the table in front of the young woman, ignoring the fact that she was on the telephone.

"I'm here to see Piper Wynne."

The woman flitted a glance over him, held up one manicured finger and got off the phone as quickly as was decent before telling him crisply, "That won't be possible."

"Look, I don't care how you make it happen, but I'm not leaving here until I see Ms. Wynne."

Frowning, the woman pecked a lavishly long fingernail against the surface of the wood desktop. "I'm afraid you have no choice."

"I'm afraid *you* have no choice," Mitch retorted. "I can have a judge on the phone inside of ten minutes, and then we'll see whether or not you can show me to Ms. Wynne's desk."

"Sir," the receptionist said, her voice taking on an edge of shrillness, "I'll be glad to point out what used to be her desk, but that's the best I can do, judge or no judge."

"Used to be?" Mitch echoed hollowly.

The young woman lowered her voice. "Ms. Wynne no longer works here."

"No longer—?" He broke off, rubbing a hand over his chin in consternation. "Where did she go? Look, this is terribly important. You might even say it's a matter of life and death. I have to see her."

The woman's manner thawed considerably, but her words were no more helpful than before. "I have no idea where she went."

He closed his eyes, one hand fisting atop the sleekly curved wood of the desk rail. "Can you find out? It's very important."

The woman hunched her shoulders and leaned forward as far as the wide counter would allow, pitching her voice low. "She wouldn't say, not even to her friends."

Mitch bowed his head. The young receptionist obviously included herself in that category.

"What's your name?" he asked softly.

"Hannah."

"If she gets in touch with you, Hannah, if you should hear anything at all, even from another employer checking references, please call me at either of those numbers on the card.''

She nodded, understanding in her eyes. ''All I know is that Piper was out sick for several days. Then she came in, said she couldn't work here anymore and left again without following protocol. Didn't even do her exit interview or collect her last paycheck. I tried to ask her what was up, but she just looked at me with tears in her eyes, shook her head and walked out again.''

Mitch sighed. ''I'm afraid she's not herself. I know she's had a terrible shock. If you see her or hear from her again, please let me know.''

Hannah cast a look right and left before whispering, ''I will.''

Mitch thanked her again and left. He was no closer to finding a solution to this problem. Indeed, the problem seemed to have grown beyond all human control. All he could think to do was to get down on his knees again.

He was halfway back to his office before he realized he had resources. He could marshal a whole army of prayer warriors with just a few phone calls.

He dialed his parents, telling them enough—it wasn't his story to tell, really—so that they could pray intelligently. Next he activated the Grief Support Group's prayer chain, again giving them just enough information so that they could phrase their petitions properly.

Finally he called the Wynnes in Houston. After he spoke to them, he knew what he had to do. It weighed on him like a two-ton millstone, but for Piper he would do whatever was necessary. Tutored by love and a God of wisdom and purpose, he could do no less.

Chapter Thirteen

Exhausted, Piper lay facedown across her bed, fully clothed. The dialysis clinic where she had taken employment kept her busy, but that wasn't the problem. The place was located in McKinney, some forty miles to the north up the busy, construction-clogged Interstate 75 corridor, also known as Central Expressway. Getting back and forth without a car was proving a real challenge. She had to change buses three times, then catch a ride with another nurse who lived in Plano.

The single mom of three was all too glad for the little bit of extra income that Piper provided, but she habitually worked a shift and a half, splitting a second shift with another nurse who came in evenings. That meant that Piper spent several hours a day just waiting for a ride back to the bus stop. She'd tried to get on the same plan as her new friend, but the company gave preference to nurses with families to support, which seemed sensible, so Piper had started making use of the exercise room that the company provided.

That, coupled with a lack of appetite lately, had caused her to drop weight, resulting in overall weakness.

Soon, she told herself, she would be toned and fit and strong again. *But not,* said a little voice inside her head, *if you don't eat properly.*

Piper sighed and rolled over, telling herself that she would get up and go to the kitchen in a moment. It was tempting to just close her eyes and pretend that tomorrow would never come. Finally, however, she bullied herself up off the bed and into the kitchen to poke her nose into the refrigerator.

She hadn't been to the grocery in over a week, and the cupboard was, quite literally, bare. She had two eggs and a slice of cheese. It would have to be an omelet, and an anemic one at that—except that as she stood staring down at the unbroken eggs, she found she wasn't quite up to the task, after all. She felt the hot, hateful prickling of tears behind her eyes, and panic set in.

Oh, God, please, not again.

As if in answer to her thoughtless prayer, a knock sounded at her door. Grateful for any distraction, she went at once to answer it. Melissa's friendly face greeted her with a tentative smile.

"Hey, stranger!" She took in Piper's violet flowered scrubs and said, "Have you changed jobs?"

"Uh, yeah, actually, I have," Piper admitted uneasily, adding, "The insurance company wasn't for me. I need more hands-on, you know?"

Melissa shrugged. "If you say so. It's certainly been keeping you busy, though. I've been missing you."

"I'm sorry." Piper apologized at once. "I just had to make some changes."

"Okay," Melissa said, eyeing her judiciously. "Have you lost weight? I thought you'd given up running."

"My new company offers an exercise room, so I've been working out there," Piper admitted with a forced smile.

"Ah. Well, listen, I've got an extra large pepperoni pizza upstairs that I could use your help with if you haven't had dinner yet. What d'you say? Scott's even promised not to rattle the glass in the windows with his music."

Piper laughed, suddenly feeling a tad better. She sensed something different about Melissa, though. Her friend seemed to have a mature new gleam in her eye—or was that concern that she saw? Either way, pepperoni pizza sounded more appetizing than eggs at the moment, especially if the eggs came with a side order of fresh tears.

"Do I have time to change?"

"Sure, if you want," Melissa said. "I'll wait."

Piper started to tell her to go on ahead, but she was suddenly ravenous. "Why not. If you don't mind the scrubs, I don't."

"Are you kidding? Every minute we're down here is another minute Scott's alone with our pie."

Laughing again, Piper promised to hurry. She felt a moment's misgiving as she grabbed her keys and walked out into the courtyard at Melissa's side. What if she suddenly burst into tears in front of her hosts? How would she ever explain it? On the other hand, she just couldn't face another lonely evening dwelling on her mistakes and losses. No, what she needed more than anything else right now was a little distraction, a little entertainment, a little fun. If *fun* no longer came as easily as it once had, well, what did, other than sorrow?

They climbed the stairs shoulder to shoulder, and when they reached Melissa's door, Melissa reached out and gave it a sharp rap before reaching for the knob. That seemed a bit odd to Piper, but the next instant Melissa swung the door open and stepped back, signaling for Piper to go in first. Piper decided that rap had been a polite way of informing Scott that they had company. Perhaps he hadn't expected Piper to actually join them. She could hardly blame him for that.

The aroma of freshly baked pizza greeted her first, and then there was Scott standing awkwardly in the middle of the floor, his hands in the back pockets of his baggy jeans.

"Hey, Piper!" he exclaimed, abruptly coming forward to hug her.

"Scott!" She didn't know whether to laugh or be alarmed by such an exuberant welcome, and then she realized that he was not the only other person in the room.

Every defense mechanism she possessed snapped to alert, but Melissa had already closed the door, and Scott's arms were still about her. Realizing with horror that she was well and truly trapped, she jerked back, a hand going to her mouth.

"Oh!"

"Hello, sis."

For one thunderstruck moment Piper could do nothing but stare at the brassy-haired man standing beside the coffee table. He looked...much the same.

That seemed wrong somehow, but welcome, too. Until she looked into his warm, reddish-brown eyes and saw reflected there the same sorrow that again threatened to tear her apart.

"I can't do this!" she wailed, but then another presence materialized at her elbow.

"Yes, you can," Mitch whispered, his strong arm coming around her shoulders.

She was desperate to believe it, and yet everything she knew about herself said it wasn't so. She wasn't strong enough to face what she'd done, what she'd lost, what she'd cost her brother and the rest of her family. She just wasn't good enough, not as good as the daughter of Ransome and Charlotte Wynne should be. And now everyone would know.

Desperately she looked to the Ninevers. "What have they told you?"

Melissa appeared on the verge of tears. "Only that your nephew died."

"In my emergency room!" Piper cried. She couldn't say, *"By my hand!"* But surely everyone else was thinking it, too.

"Is that why you ran from us, Pip?" Gordon asked, using her old childhood nickname. Of course he had to know that it was.

Trembling, she stood and watched Gordon approach. Only when he stopped did she realize that he carried something in his hand. Then he turned out his palm, and she was looking down into the smiling face of her nephew Asia. It was too much. She tried to twist away—to run, even—but Mitch's long, strong arm wouldn't let her.

"Wait," he whispered. "Listen."

"He was so much like you," Gordon said, and

Piper looked up sharply, hearing the note of pride in his voice. "Sunny-natured, caring, quick to take responsibility for everyone else's happiness."

"No," she said, even as her gaze fell once more on that beloved face. "No." The tears started to run again, but not so heavily that she couldn't see Asia's impish smile. "He was so good. He never complained."

"Neither do you," Gordon said, lifting his free hand to her shoulder.

"Inside," she confessed brokenly. "You don't know how many complaints I've kept inside."

"Yes, I do," he insisted gently, "I always knew, and I've always admired you for your restraint. I've struggled so hard to be more like you, Pip, always thinking of others, putting yourself last. Don't you know that?"

That made so little sense that she shook her head. "No."

"Can't imagine why I'd want to be like you?" Gordon smiled, gazing down at the photo in his hand. "Just think of Asia and you'll know. As I said, he was like you."

Piper shook her head again. "If only you knew," she choked out.

"But I do, sis," Gordon went on. "Now, Thai...Thai is like me. He has to learn everything the hard way, always sure he's doing the right thing no matter what anyone else says. Quick to complain, to lash out."

"You're not like that," Piper scoffed, dashing away tears. He was a wonderful brother, father, husband, a wonderful pastor. He didn't deserve to lose his firstborn son.

"You don't know," he said gently, "because Mom and Dad never complained about me." Tucking the photo into a pocket, he grasped her by both shoulders. "Pip, why do you think you wound up in boarding school?"

"I—I don't know." But it was something to think about, a way to fix her attention. "T-to get an education."

Gordon shook his head. "It was to protect you, to insure that you didn't make the mistakes that I did."

"No, you were just a little high-spirited," she insisted.

"Rebellious," he corrected. "Always getting into trouble, running with thugs. You remember the Thai gangs. I was particularly intrigued by a bunch called the Red Dagger." He chuckled lightly. "It was rumored that you had to kill someone to get in. I'm not sure it was true, but I told myself that I was willing."

"Gordon, you could never hurt anyone," she admonished, holding herself together with that familiar tone and attitude. He smiled at her in that grateful, protective, indulgent way of his.

"Probably not," he admitted, "but I so hated being different that I almost convinced myself that I could. When Mom and Dad found out I was hanging around with the Red Dagger bunch, they shipped me off to boarding school so fast that my head was spinning. You were, what, three and a half, four years old?"

Piper nodded, remembering well how she'd sobbed when he'd left them. A winsome thought curled her mouth into a self-deprecating half smile. "I never minded the idea of boarding school because I always thought you'd be there. When I found out you wouldn't be, I was so disappointed."

"I know. Mom told me. Why do you think I spent all those weekends with you?" Gordon looked down and said in a soft, agonized voice, "I used to tell Asia that he was as important to his brother as you were to me. That was one of the reasons he tried to slip out of the house that night."

Suddenly plummeted back into the chasm of loss, Piper shook her head. "No, no, that can't be right."

"He was following his brother," Gordon explained gently. "Thai had slipped out that same way a little while earlier. He was going to meet some boys who are known around school as bad kids, boys we'd forbidden him to hang out with, and Asia wanted to stop him without his mother and me finding out. He left a note saying that he was going to your place. I guess he figured you could help him find Thai and talk him out of doing anything stupid."

Piper closed her eyes, barely able to take it all in. "Poor Thai," she whispered. He was almost as guilty as she.

"Unfortunately, Thai is lighter than his brother," Gordon said calmly. "When Asia tried to climb down the ivy trellis as Thai had done, it gave way."

She covered her ears with her hands. "Oh, no."

"He hit the decorative lamp in the yard on his way down," Gordon told her matter-of-factly. "It was a freak accident, Pip, just two stories and a wrought-iron gas lamp on a pole. The thing was no bigger than his head."

Piper cried out. How unfair! How cruel! Why would God let something like that happen? But no, she couldn't escape her guilt that easily.

"He didn't have to die!" she wailed.

"It was nobody's fault, Pip," he argued gently.

"You don't know what I did!" she gasped, trembling head to toe.

"You tried to save his life," Gordon insisted.

"I ordered them to take off the collar! I made the decision to incise instead of going through his mouth! If I hadn't done that the convulsions wouldn't have dislodged the bone shards!"

"You don't know that."

"I do know it! I read the coroner's report!"

"Including the part that said his neck was broken?"

"Yes!"

"And the part that said the concussion alone was enough to kill him?"

Piper blinked at him. "What?"

"All the medical personnel said that you couldn't have known how severe the concussion was. The doctor suspected it, but even he didn't know for sure until after the coroner made his report."

He was probably dead when you popped that collar.

When, not *because.*

Was it possible that she wasn't responsible?

No, of course not. That would mean God had allowed her sweet, good nephew to die.

"I didn't even know it was him!" she cried. "I didn't even recognize my own nephew. He was on *my* table in *my* cube and I didn't even know!"

"There wasn't time," Gordon argued. "His face was lacerated and horribly swollen. You were preoccupied with trying to save his life! How can you blame yourself for that? Oh, Pip, forgive me for not realizing what you were going through until it was too late!"

Piper reeled back. "Forgive *you?* You lost your son! *I* should have saved him. It was my job to save him! I'm the one who doesn't deserve forgiveness. I'm the one who—" What? she wondered wildly. Unable to think clearly anymore, she turned and would have fled if Mitch hadn't suddenly sidestepped into her path and seized her by both shoulders, shaking her none too gently.

"Who on earth do you think you are? The one person in the world whom God can't forgive? What is it that makes you so important? Do you really believe that because you're Ransome and Charlotte Wynne's daughter that even God measures you by a higher standard than everyone else? Talk about arrogance! And believe me, I know arrogance when I run into it. I've bumped up against my own often enough!"

Piper blinked. "What?" Mitch, arrogant? Not the Mitch she knew. But maybe that was the point.

"I once thought I was the savior of every unfortunate soul who stumbled across my path," he told her sternly. "I was more understanding, more generous, more forgiving, more just, more *everything* than the next defense attorney. Then a drunk driver plowed into my wife's car and killed her on impact, and I blamed myself because I had once defended that drunk driver in court! I had made a career of defending the indefensible. My wife was dead, and it was my fault, period."

"Oh, Mitch."

"It didn't matter to me that I hadn't even gotten him off the first offense." Mitch drew back and rubbed one hand over his face, the other going to his hip. "The guy served a year and even went through counseling, but he was a drunk. I couldn't lay it all on him. And I couldn't blame God. What was my faith worth, ultimately, if my God is not a God of love who always has my best interests at heart? It couldn't be just an accident, and it couldn't be for anyone's benefit, so someone had to be to blame, and that someone had to be *me.*"

"But you didn't do anything wrong," Piper said, believing it wholeheartedly.

"I know that now," he agreed, "but at the time I had to be guilty because focusing on my guilt kept me from facing my wife's death."

Piper jerked as if he'd struck her. Was that what she was doing, hiding from loss, from grief, by punishing herself?

"My in-laws finally made me see how arrogant and pointless that was," he went on. "Do you know, they went to see that drunk driver in jail to forgive him, and to make sure that he knew God was willing to forgive him, too? It took me three whole years to forgive him because first I had to forgive myself. Only then could I really grieve. Everything before that, all the tears and recriminations and self-punishment, was a waste."

Piper closed her eyes. That couldn't be true. That would mean all the tears she had shed thus far, all the agony and worthlessness she'd been feeling were for nothing.

"Real guilt—not always the consequences, but the guilt—can be dealt with in an instant," Mitch was saying. "You realize what you've done wrong, make up your mind not to do it again, and confess it to God." He snapped his fingers. "Over and done with. Doesn't even exist anymore."

She opened her eyes hopefully at that. The Bible did say, quite clearly and repeatedly, that God not only forgave but forgot confessed sin, and yet her repeated confession had brought her only deeper sorrow. She'd started to think that she was unforgivable. Was it possible that she'd confessed imaginary sins?

"False guilt," Mitch went on, "is conjured up out of emotion, and until we're willing and able to face those emotions and get to the real reasons for it, we're just stuck with it."

Piper lifted a hand to her eyes, realizing that she had been blind to the real problem all along. She hadn't grieved. She hadn't let go of Asia at all. Instead she'd clung tight to guilt, anything that could keep her from facing the truth, the pain of actual loss. It hit her like a fist to the solar plexus then, literally doubling her over.

Both Mitch and Gordon were at her side in an instant. Strong, loving arms enveloped her from every direction. She began to weep as she had never wept before, not even in these past painful weeks, but this time she didn't even try to fight it. Instead she let the horrible realizations wash over her.

Asia was gone from this world. She had spent his last moments in it with him—working to keep him here, even though she hadn't known it was him. Despite her best efforts and for reasons she couldn't begin to understand, God had taken Asia anyway. She would never again walk into her brother's house and see Asia's smiling welcome, never listen to him carefully working out his concerns, never make him laugh or hear him pray or watch him grow to maturity. Never.

Not in this life.

She screamed, anguish wrenching the sound from her chest, and for some time afterward she didn't know anything other than the comforting strength of those supporting her.

Eventually she realized she was being guided, aware only of the supportive arms about her and the strong, solid shoulder upon which she rested her head. Awash in grief, she heard voices in quick, stilted conversation but couldn't register the words. Carefully coaxed, she moved her feet in mechanical response until she had reached her own apartment and was lowered tenderly into a sitting position.

She wept for a very long while—it seemed like days, but turned out to be only hours—cocooned in a comforting embrace and hateful loss, until at last the shell began to crumble and awful clarity began to return.

"Asia," she gasped, at last grasping the finality of his passing.

"I know, I know," Gordon said, appearing at eye level and taking her hands, "but he did what he set out to do, Pip."

"Thai?" she asked shakily, her concern for him suddenly as strong as her grief for Asia.

"Is going to be fine," Gordon assured her. "He's had a rough time of it, but he's getting help."

Feeling immense relief at that, she briefly closed her eyes. "I'm glad."

"Pip, I know he accused you that day," Gordon said gently, rubbing the backs of her hands with his thumbs, "but he didn't mean it. That was his own guilt talking. He desperately needed someone else to blame."

"I know," she whispered brokenly.

Gordon reached up to clap a hand around the nape of her neck. "Sis, please believe me, none of us ever dreamed that you took him seriously or even that you blamed yourself. I did hear what you said about having the collar removed, but I guess I thought that was just your effort to absolve Thai of his own guilt."

Her chin began to wobble. "All I could think about was that being Asia in there and my not even knowing and not being able to save him and if I'd made the right decisions and how would I go on without..."

Gordon pulled her upper body forward into his arms. "Oh, Pip, I'm so sorry."

"No, no. You've done nothing."

"I didn't see how alone you were in your grief, how you blamed yourself."

"You were grieving, too."

"I still am. Part of me always will, just as part of Thai will always feel responsible for what happened to Asia." He set her back then, looking her squarely in the eye. "But we all understand, even Thai now, that God allowed this to happen for a reason. Thai believes that out of this must come a great purpose for his own life. He's just waiting for God to show him what that is."

A great purpose, Piper thought, and her gaze turned automatically to Mitch, who sat at her side. Somehow she'd known that was where he'd be, that those were his arms in which she'd found refuge, his shoulder upon which she'd leaned, cried. It seemed entirely appropriate. Mitch, after all, had found purpose in his life due to loss, and so would Thai, and so must she. So must they all.

"Maybe you could talk to him," she suggested hopefully.

"I would be honored to," he replied thickly, "but Thai already has an excellent counselor in his corner."

"But you have personal experience."

"So does Thai's counselor, honey. It's one of the prerequisites. Besides, I can't tell Thai, or you, what God's purpose is in this. No one can. But I promise you that it exists, and that it will be enough to sustain him and you, even to bring joy again eventually, though I know you can't conceive of such a thing just now."

"It almost seems wrong to think about joy at a time like this," she conceded.

"Well, it isn't," Gordon assured her. "Just as there is a joy that surpasses understanding, so is there a joy that abides where joy cannot exist, a joy entirely of God and our personal relationships with Him."

"You're absolutely right," Mitch said, "but living to God's purpose is never easy. I'm not sure it's even supposed to be, because if it were, we'd just become complacent about His guidance." Mitch looked to Gordon again and added, "Your letter is a case in point. I knew there was a reason I found it, but finding anyone connected to it seemed impossible, even after the airline agreed to help. And then I let—" he glanced at Piper "—personal considerations get in the way, though maybe that was the entire point." He shook his head. "All I know is, God works these things out, not me, and the only thing more difficult than living to God's purpose is *not* living to God's purpose."

"Your letter," Piper whispered to her brother, stricken. "I didn't even read it."

"That's okay. You'll read it when you're ready."

"Maybe you'd like to read it now," Mitch suggested gently. "I'll get it for you if you'll tell me where it is."

She wiped her face with both hands, a fruitless exercise, as the tears had slowed but wouldn't yet be stemmed. Still, the gesture felt strengthening somehow. "Top right drawer of the bureau in my bedroom."

Mitch nodded and rose, moving silently into the other room. Gordon smiled compassionately and swept a hand over her head in a familiar gesture of affection.

"I'm so sorry that I didn't see the shape you were in sooner, Pip. You were such a rock for the rest of us, and we let you down."

She shook her head, chest shuddering with an indrawn breath. "I thought I'd let *you* down, and I was sure you all knew it."

"Believe me, that was the last thing we thought. When I heard that you'd sold your car and were giving things away, I couldn't imagine what was going on. You weren't answering the phone or the door. By the time I realized that you were leaving town, you had completely cut yourself off from the rest of us. I was so worried, and then in the middle of a long, restless night, I felt this impulse to write down everything I wanted to say to you."

"And here it is," Mitch said, reappearing with the letter, including the crumpled middle page that he'd returned to her.

When she'd found the letter pinned to her front door that day, she'd simply stuck it into her handbag unopened. Then as she was searching for her boarding pass at the airport, she'd come across it again, and for a moment she'd yielded to the impulse to read it, but once she'd slit the envelope with her fingernail, removed the sheets inside and thumbed through them, panic had set in. She'd hastily tried to stuff it all back into the envelope, but she'd wound up with the pages out of order and at least one of them folded separately.

Apparently she hadn't gotten it back in the envelope at all but had tucked it loose, with the envelope containing the other sheets, into the outside pocket of her purse. It must have slipped out as she was on her way to board the plane. She remembered now that some guy had tried to talk to her in the gangway, but it was noisy in that confined space with everyone rushing to get on the plane. It had seemed an inappropriate time to stop and chat, so she'd pretty much ignored him. She wondered now if he hadn't been trying to tell her that she'd dropped something.

As she took the envelope into her hands once more, she knew that she hadn't been meant to read the letter until this moment. God had other purposes in mind when He'd had Gordon write down these words all those weeks ago. Surely it was no accident that Mitch, of all people, had found the sheet of paper on the ground that day. Feeling her first moment of real strength since her nephew had passed from this world to the next, Piper unfolded the pages and began to read.

Chapter Fourteen

"**M**y darling sister,

"I was almost twelve years old when you were born, and you were but a couple of years younger when God gave us Asia. You have both always been miracles to me, the baby sister I had stopped expecting to have, the son I only dreamed of having. You were such a little thing when Mom and Dad shipped me off to school, and I was far too manly at fifteen to admit how badly I was going to miss you. It was selfish of me to be so glad when they decided that you should have an American education, too.

"As a father myself at that point, I understood the sacrifice that Mom and Dad were making on your behalf and had made earlier for me. You don't know how often I've thanked God that He did not require such sacrifice from me! I never dreamed what He would one day require or imagine that I could survive what He would ask of me. And yet, God remains all goodness, and I will not only survive but thrive. I really believe that now, and why shouldn't I?

"What a gift Asia was and is! Just the thought of him is almost too painful to be borne just now, but our love of him will surely never subside, and will one day be, not a cross to bear, but a cherished joy. His memory will sustain us until that time, and that's why it is so important that we not forget. The pain makes us want, in its depth and rawness, to do just that, but to forget our dear boy would be to rob us of all the delights he brought into our lives.

"Hold on to that, dear heart. Don't let him go, for if you do, you also let me go, and how can I bear that? To lose you as well as him is more, surely, than God can allow, so I beg you, please don't leave. I need you. We all need you. How he would hate it if he thought that his loss would tear this family apart!

"Whatever you do, please know that I love you. I don't blame you in any way. You will always be my treasured little sister, not a baby anymore but a woman with so much to offer those who suffer! But you are suffering now. I'm so sorry that I didn't realize how much. In my sorrow, I selfishly took of your strength. We all did. Perhaps we always have, and your leaving will force us all to rely finally and completely on God alone. If that is so, Pip, then I take back my plea. Go if you must, sweet girl, but come back to us soon. I promise we'll appreciate you more.

"If I've never told you how proud I am of you, Pip, then let me do so now. We know how hard you worked to save Asia, how hard you work to save all your patients—and how often you are successful! I'm glad for Asia that you were in the room when his spirit departed his body. He deserved the best, and that's what he, we, always got, always will have, with you.

"So if you must go, go with God, and know that the love and prayers of your family are with you, too. That includes Asia, I am sure, and how I praise God for it! And for you.

"In Him, your loving brother,"

It was signed "Gordo."

Piper let the letter fall to her lap and reached for her brother with both arms. How could she have hidden herself away from such love? He didn't blame her. He had always trusted, had always understood, that she had tried her best for Asia, even when she hadn't known that it was him on that gurney.

Why had she believed she had lost everything? In reality she had lost only one member of her family and only for the remainder of her time here on earth. It was no small thing, to lose that time with a loved one, and yet the promise of reunification in heaven was real, as real as the brother she held in her arms, as real as the man who, in obedience to his personal mission and God's will, was bringing love back into her life when she would have banished it forever.

Looking up at Mitch, she reached out one hand and tried to tell him with her grip that she understood now, or at least that she was starting to understand.

"Thank you," she whispered brokenly. "Thank you."

He just smiled and bowed his head. Piper and Gordon naturally followed suit, and as easily as breathing, they went together to God, for comfort, for forgiveness, for understanding and wisdom, for direction, for peace, but most important of all, in genuine gratitude.

Mitch had never felt so torn. On one hand, he knew without doubt that he had done the right thing in calling Piper's brother and forcing the issue. Already the healing had begun. As always, it was a joy to see, but this time the joy was especially bittersweet and the satisfaction had a dark, sharp side to it. In doing what was best for Piper, he might well have dashed his own personal dreams and hopes. Telling himself that God had only his best interests at heart in this, too, helped, but not as much as it should have.

It was easiest just to keep busy, holding at bay thoughts of the future, and as usual, he found plenty to do. For one thing, the Ninevers deserved to be kept abreast of the situation, and for another, Piper desperately needed to eat. He'd been shocked to see how much weight she'd lost in less than two weeks! Thankfully, when he asked if she'd like him to get in something for dinner, she'd shot him a wan smile and suggested somewhat mischievously, "Pizza?"

He now had no doubt about her idea of comfort food, at least. Chuckling, he'd left her in the capable hands of her brother, with whom he seemed to share a natural ease, and went out to fulfill her request. He knew exactly how to manage it. After climbing the stairs, he knocked at the door of the Ninevers' apartment. Melissa opened the door at once.

"How is she?"

"Better."

"Thank God!"

Mitch smiled to hear the words tumble so effortlessly from her mouth. "And thank you, too."

She waved that away with a flip of her hand. "Does she need anything?"

"Pizza."

Both Scott, who sat on the floor in front of the coffee table, and Melissa seemed momentarily taken aback, but then they began to smile. When Melissa had hit upon the pizza invitation, she'd insisted that she actually intended to feed her friend pizza, so it wasn't a lie, even if it was a trick.

"It'll need warming," she warned, heading for the kitchen.

"No problem," he told her, rocking back on his heels.

Scott got up and came to lean on the back of the couch. "What's going to happen now?" he asked.

Mitch felt his smile fade. "I don't know for sure."

"She's going back to Houston, isn't she?" Melissa asked from the dining area, pizza box in hand.

Mitch found that he had to swallow before he could answer. "She should." But he couldn't help hoping that she wouldn't.

Nevertheless, when Piper turned to him a couple hours later—after dining quietly on microwaved pizza and seesawing back and forth between uneasy joy and sudden sorrow—with very nearly the same question as Scott, Mitch gave her very nearly the same answer.

"I know what needs to happen next, Piper." He saw the trust in her beautiful amber eyes and reached down deep for the will to do what was best for her. "You should go home to Houston and join Gordon and the rest of your family in grief counseling."

She bowed her head at that, her hands tucked away beneath the small table around which they sat in her dining area. Mitch glanced at Gordon and saw a wealth of understanding in his serene expression.

"You're right," she said finally, and the tight, brittle sound of her voice perfectly reflected the state of his heart. She sighed and lifted her chin. "You can run from grief, but you can't hide."

He smiled, aching with a growing sense of loss. "It took me three years to learn that lesson."

"I don't know how you managed to cope for three years," she told him softly. "I'm exhausted after three months." Her eyes filled with tears again. He knew that they would come unbidden at the drop of a hat for a while. But he wouldn't be there to dry them for her.

"You're not as stubborn as I am," he said softly, trying—and failing—to lighten the mood.

"It's a shame we can't counsel with you," Gordon said, but Mitch shook his head.

"I'm too personally involved."

"Yes," Gordon murmured, "I suspect you are."

Mitch looked up, and once more the two men joined in a moment of absolute clarity. Finally Mitch looked away and cleared his throat.

"You need to get some rest. I should go now."

"I suspect tomorrow will be a busy day," Gordon commented, and Mitch pushed back his chair. Gordon did the same a heartbeat later. For a moment Piper seemed too tired even to try to get up from the table, but then she straightened her shoulders and rose.

Mitch selfishly let her walk him to the door. It was only feet away. Still, she had weathered a great emotional storm that evening and it wasn't over yet, though he suspected, prayed for her sake, that the worst had passed. They paused together.

"Mitch," she began, shaking her head, "I don't know how to—"

"Hush," he interrupted, knowing her thanks would be misplaced. "You just concentrate on yourself and your family for now. God will take care of everything else, especially me.''

"Will you stay in touch with Melissa and Scott?''

"Absolutely. I'll see them every Sunday, at least. Scott says they'll be joining church soon.''

At that she closed her eyes, hands clasped against her chest. "I'm so glad.''

"You see, good has already come of this.''

She smiled through her tears. "It has, hasn't it?''

He nodded and heard himself promise, "The best is yet to come. You'll see.''

"Will I?'' she asked. Then, before he could answer, "Will you?''

He knew what she was asking, but he wasn't sure how to answer. His own fear was that his part in her life was finished. Now that he had accomplished his purpose, his mission, he had no more excuse to remain close to her. Gordon was right about God having a reason for all that He allowed into the lives of His children, but Mitch knew that he was correct when he'd told them both that no one could predict that purpose. Considering the way God had used Piper and her family thus far, he couldn't rule out the possibility that she would one day soon find herself called to the foreign mission field. With her nursing ability, it seemed a strong possibility to him. It seemed improbable that God would ask the same thing of him, though. He had important work right here in Dallas.

Finally he managed to say, "We'll leave that all up to God.''

For a long moment she stood staring up at him through her tears, supplication evident on her face, but he couldn't give her the assurances she seemed to want. He couldn't even assure himself that she

would still want them in a few weeks. As if coming
to the same conclusion, she bit her lip, nodded and
reached out a hand to him.

He took her into his arms, perhaps for the last time,
and held on so tightly that he was sure, once he finally
managed to tear himself away, that he would forever
carry her imprint on his heart.

Piper couldn't quite believe that she was going. Intellectually she knew that Mitch was right when he
said she needed to return to Houston and join her
family in grief counseling. Yet a part of her no longer
recognized Houston as home. Then again, this apartment was not home, either, though she had lived here
for months. She knew that without any doubt as she
stood in the open doorway surveying it all for the last
time.

Had it been only two days since she'd climbed
those stairs expecting pizza, only to find her brother—
and healing—waiting for her? She checked her watch.
Not even two whole days, as it was only about two
o'clock in the afternoon. They would be back in
Houston before seven. It seemed impossible that it
should be so, yet her bags had been packed and were
even now being stowed in the trunk of Gordon's car.

Mitch had used his legal expertise to get her out of
the apartment lease, citing familial hardship, and the
landlord had been kind enough to agree to return her
deposit. The rental agency would come around to pick
up the furniture soon. She'd resigned her third job in
as many months by saying simply that a family death
necessitated her immediate return to Houston, and
Melissa had agreed to call Hannah at the insurance
company and explain in whatever fashion she felt best

why Piper had left things there as she had. Piper suspected that the two women would get along well, perhaps even become friends, especially after Melissa had wondered aloud whether she should invite Hannah to church.

Piper smiled to herself. Good had come of this tragedy, perhaps more than she would ever know. She would never have chosen to meet the Ninevers, Hannah, or even Mitch in this fashion, and she couldn't with good reason say she had been the agent for any blessing that might have come to any of them through knowing her. Yet good had resulted.

The Ninevers were in church and growing in their relationship with God. Hannah, and who knew how many others, might well be influenced because of them. Mitch had fulfilled his mission; God had channeled blessing and healing through him as surely as water flowed through a pipe. Apparently even Thai had benefited, harsh as the lesson had been, from what had happened. Only time would tell what the results of that would be, but Gordon seemed to feel that Thai had turned an important corner. If that were so, then in anything that Thai accomplished during his life Asia would have a hand.

The thought comforted more than it grieved, and that was a good thing, too.

Only in one regard was Piper unsure. How could she let go of Mitch? Somehow without her even knowing it, he had become her anchor. No, it was more than that.

Now, when she thought of home, it wasn't Houston or Dallas or houses or apartments that she thought of; it was Mitch. And yet she couldn't stay here. She knew that as certainly as she knew her own name.

Sighing, she closed the apartment door behind her. "Is that everything, then?"

She turned at the sound of Mitch's voice. He looked very dear standing there—big, strong, handsome. Right. His serene smile both gladdened and worried her. To cover the latter, she adjusted the strap of her handbag on her shoulder. Could he really let her go so easily? She pushed the thought aside and answered his question.

"I think so."

"Well, then." He offered his arm.

She felt an instant's letdown, but then she squared her shoulders, disciplined her disquiet and slipped her hand around the curve of his elbow, allowing him to escort her toward the security gate and the front parking area, which was actually closer to the apartment than the residents' parking lot.

"It was good of you to come to see us off," she said after taking a moment to further compose herself. "I know you're busy."

"You didn't imagine that I would let you leave without saying goodbye, surely. After all, I was the first to welcome you to Dallas. I reserve the right to be the last to let you go home to Houston again."

"Houston isn't home," she said, echoing the earlier thought.

"No? Where is, then? You said the same about Thailand once, as I recall."

Home is wherever you are, she thought, but she wasn't brash enough to say it aloud. Something of her thoughts must have shown on her face, however, for he quickly looked away.

"Have you seen Melissa and Scott today?" he asked, casually changing the subject.

She shook her head and targeted her gaze on the path that her feet followed by rote. "I said my good-byes to them yesterday, and I don't want to have to do it again."

"I understand."

Trying to think her way through to any loose ends, she suddenly remembered something. "You never told me about the doctor's case."

"It's not resolved yet. Any time you get the State Department involved, you can expect a lengthy litigation, but I suspect it will come out all right in the end. Meanwhile, my client's been offered a job in hospital administration. It's not what he really should be doing, but at least it's medicine."

"Will you tell him that I'm praying for him?" Piper asked impulsively, and was rewarded with a warm smile.

"I'll be glad to. You're not alone in that, by the way. My mother's rallied a veritable army of prayer warriors on his behalf, and frankly, Dad was instrumental in getting him that job."

"I didn't expect less," Piper told him truthfully, but then she stopped and looked up at him. "About your parents, Mitch. I don't know what you've told them."

"Everything," he said flatly. "I always do." His lips quirked. "Eventually."

Her brow furrowed. "I hope they don't think—"

"They think their prayers for you have been answered," he interrupted softly. "Not that they, we, won't be praying for you in the future. We most assuredly will."

She looked up at him helplessly, trying to tell him with her eyes what she dared not put into words. Finally she tried to say what he hadn't really let her say so far.

"Mitch, I owe you so much."

"Now, now, none of that."

"No, please, it's important that you let me say this."

He dropped his gaze, but then he nodded. "All right."

"When I first met you," she began, "I sensed...well, that you were a danger to me, or rather to my very carefully constructed house of cards."

"Piper, please believe me," he said. "I never meant to hurt you."

"You didn't," she hastily assured him, squeezing his arm. "Just the opposite. You saved me from myself." He was shaking his head, but she pressed the point. "Mitch, I was running blind, and I was headed straight for a brick wall, and you were the one person who saw the signs, the one person uniquely qualified to see them."

"But that's just it, honey. God engineered this thing. I didn't go looking for you. He shoved me right into your path."

"I know that, and I'm not diminishing His hand in this, but you were willing, Mitch. You *are* willing to be used by God. Thank you. Not just for myself but on behalf of all those who are blessed by your willingness to let God work through you."

He didn't seem to know what to say to that. He even seemed a little embarrassed by it. She took pity on him. Going up on tiptoe, she wrapped her free arm around him, pulling his head down to hers, and kissed his cheek.

They stood locked in an awkward embrace for long

moments before he whispered, "I'm going to miss you so much."

Heartened, Piper pulled back in order to search his face, but he wouldn't quite meet her gaze. "Mitch," she began urgently, "you once said that you loved me. If you still—"

He pressed a finger to her lips, cutting off the flow of words. "This is best, Piper. You have to go with Gordon. You can't be thinking of anything right now but of getting through to the other side."

"The other side?"

He dropped both hands to her shoulders, cupping the tops of her arms. "Grief is like a deep, dark canyon. You know in the twenty-third Psalm where it talks about the valley of the shadow of death? Well, I think that's talking about grief, the shadow that falls on us all when someone we love no longer inhabits this world with us. It's like walking through a dark, scary canyon all alone without any idea where we're going, but God is always right there with us, and if we just keep going, just keep working our way through, we'll come out on the other side and once more find that our cups are overflowing with blessings. I've done all I can to point you in the right direction, sweetheart. Now it's up to you to take the hand that God is offering and let Him guide you through to the other side."

Piper gulped, knowing that he was right, and nodded her understanding. "I will, but Mitch, what if, when I get there, what if…" *You're not* were the words she couldn't say.

He met her gaze and held it with his. "Only God knows where you'll come out, Piper. If I did know, I'd try to find a way to be there."

For a brief moment her heart soared. "Oh, Mitch."

"But that may not be what God has in mind," he warned. "You have to know that and accept it."

"Have you?" she asked, her tremulous voice just a little above a whisper.

"I'm trying," he answered in kind.

There was nothing else, then. As much as she might want Mitch to ask her to stay, neither of them could be disobedient to God in this. She closed her eyes and burrowed once more into his arms, her head upon his shoulder.

"I love you, too," she whispered in such a small voice that he couldn't possibly have heard. It was an honor to say it, though, to give the thought free rein finally.

Gordon broke them apart by clearing his throat.

"You about ready there, sis?"

She dashed hot tears from her eyes and turned to face him with as much determination as she could muster.

"Ready."

She went swiftly to let herself into the car while he shook hands and exchanged quiet words with Mitch. Gazing at him through the windshield, she lifted a hand in reluctant farewell, but Mitch just stood there with his hands in his pockets while Gordon settled himself behind the steering wheel, started the sedan and shifted the transmission into gear. Without warning, Gordon sent the car swiftly backward into the street, taking advantage of a break in traffic, and then he shifted again, starting them forward even as he turned the wheel sharply to the right.

Piper closed her eyes to keep from looking back. Tears leaked from beneath them, and she knew with sad resignation that they weren't going to stop any time soon.

Chapter Fifteen

November in Houston was a lovely time. While most of the rest of the country lived in the sleepy barrenness of the end of autumn, the Houston area basked in mellow sunshine and shirt-sleeve temperatures. Without the vicious heat of summertime to boil the humidity into steam, the dampness seemed verdant rather than wilting and carried with it a real sense of the ocean, though the Gulf Coast lay almost an hour farther south. It had always been Piper's favorite time to live in Houston, but she cared little for it this year.

Asia was not there to enjoy it with the family, and so it was less enjoyable. It was the same with everything. No day was quite what it would have been if he had been there to share it. No activity, however mundane, felt as it once had. The harsh fact that Asia had been but never would be again part of the physical picture colored every memory.

Yet, little by little, a different joy began to bind the

family together, the joy of having known and nurtured Asia Wynne.

Another joy was also growing. It grew with Thai, matured as he did, blossomed as he did, tentatively at first, the bud of possibility closing tight whenever a shadow passed but furling open a little more every time the sun shone. It began to reveal itself in an opulent rose of surpassing beauty.

Asia had once taken the lead in church youth activities, had once been the most comfortable to stand and pray aloud, to talk about God's goodness and love. But Asia had not known what Thai now knew, the all-encompassing richness of God's forgiveness. Asia had not needed such forgiveness in his short life. His personality and his predisposition had not required such largesse from the God Who loved and treasured him. Thai's did, and the more God poured out His forgiveness, love and strength, the more Thai soaked it up.

"He'll take the pulpit one day and put me deep in the shadow," Gordon commented one Sunday after a youth worship service at which Thai had spoken.

"Both of us," Ransome agreed. "I see a powerful evangelism developing there."

"God has purpose for each of us," Charlotte observed sagely, "and fulfilling His purpose is satisfaction enough."

Piper agreed wholeheartedly, and yet her own purpose eluded her.

"Be patient," her sister-in-law, Jeanette, advised. "God's timing is perfect, you know."

She did know. How could she doubt? And yet, worry did intrude upon the process—often at first, then less as time went by and November yielded its beauty to the soggy chill of December.

The family pressed her not to work, and she really had no urgent reason to, at least not right away. She'd moved in with her parents and was enjoying just being their daughter again. Almost immediately upon her return, she'd leased her house to a young couple expecting their first child, and the rental payment covered the small mortgage with plenty to spare for her personal needs. Plus, she still had some savings, despite having had to make both the rent on her apartment and the mortgage on her little house. She'd never tried to replace her car.

She could afford to take her time deciding what to do next, what she was meant to do next, and yet she couldn't quite escape an uncomfortable feeling of suspended animation. It was as if her life were on hold.

As the determination to survive and heal took root and began to outpace grief, the latter began to shrivel and wither. And still Piper didn't know what her purpose was. She considered again the possibility of getting her master's degree. Houston boasted some fine programs, but it was the nursing school of the Texas Women's University of Dallas that drew her. She put off registering, uncertain about her own motivations. Mitch was in Dallas, and she hadn't heard a single word from him since she'd left there.

She'd written to him a few times, three to be exact, but when he hadn't answered, she had stopped. From time to time she considered picking up the telephone, but in the end she couldn't bring herself to do it. If he wasn't in touch because he didn't want to be, she'd rather not know. If it was for some other reason, she trusted that it was valid.

When she let herself, she was hurt by Mitch's silence, but in truth, her focus remained on getting through what he'd identified as "the valley of the shadow of death." The counseling had proven a great comfort and help, but lately in group session she found herself doing more ministering to others than being ministered to. That, she supposed correctly, was progress, but it did little to resolve her growing restlessness.

Christmas was difficult. The first Christmas without Asia was more a time of tears than merriment, and yet the *meaning* of Christmas seemed particularly poignant that year. Gordon and Jeanette gave Thai a special gift, his brother's Bible. No one was surprised when he declared with quiet conviction that he would put it to good use. Later he confided privately to Piper, as Asia might once have done, that he had known for some time that God was calling him to ministry but that he'd refused to yield to that call until lately.

"I just didn't want to do it," he confessed with more quiet strength and forthrightness than any fourteen-year-old could naturally possess. "Then right after...I knew that I didn't deserve a career in ministry."

"No one does, Thai," Piper pointed out gently.

He nodded. "I know, not on our own, but God can make us worthy through His grace and use us anyway if we let Him."

"You're exactly right," she told him, thinking of Mitch, who had allowed God to use him even when the price must have seemed far too steep.

"You know what the other part of it was?" he

asked sheepishly. "I mean, why I didn't want to be in official ministry?"

"Why was that?"

"I didn't want my kids to be preacher's kids."

She had to laugh. She put her arm around him, and they laughed about it together. "It'll serve them right, don't you think?"

"Yeah, probably. That's what I'm afraid of."

"You know what they say about paying for your raising," she teased, and they both sobered. Sometimes others paid, too.

"You know what I keep thinking, Aunt Pip?"

"What, honey?"

"That if God had said to Asia, 'You have to do this for your brother,' he'd have said, 'Okay. Sure.'"

"Oh, Thai," she whispered, hugging him close, "what a gift that is, to know that he loved you that much!"

"Loves me," Thai corrected with absolute conviction. "That's the thing. Real love never dies."

Real love never dies. *Real* love.

She later found herself thinking about that. Often. Usually when she thought of Mitch. But still the days passed without any communication from him.

The New Year came.

Thankfully, the event was not as somber as Christmas had been only a week earlier. It was as if the New Year brought with it a new era in all of their lives. Perhaps it was not entirely welcome, but all were willing to embrace it, knowing that was what Asia would want and expect of them.

Winter or what passed for it in Houston, Texas, had taken up residence, but the days seemed less gray to Piper, less shadowed. She began to think seriously of returning to work, her restlessness growing with the passage of time. She decided to tell the family when they gathered at Gordon and Jeanette's on the first Sunday in February to mark her twenty-seventh birthday.

When she walked into the house that afternoon, accompanied by her parents, she found the place full of streamers and balloons. The whole family seemed in a truly festive mood, so much that she was happy to have given them a reason to celebrate. Jeanette had ordered a cake—Piper's favorite, chocolate—and Charlotte had picked up the ice cream to go with it. As Charlotte handed over the round carton in the dining room, Jeanette took a look at the lid and remarked, "Pistachio. Asia would have loved that."

"Hey!" Thai protested jokingly. "You couldn't get my favorite?"

"I thought it was your favorite, too," Ransome said, brow furrowing as he peeled off his jacket.

"It is," Thai admitted with a grin. "You don't expect me to always let Asia get top billing, do you? What kind of pesky kid brother would I be if I did that?"

"Oh, you!" Jeanette scolded fondly, chucking him under the chin. "Just for that, you have to bring in the plates and flatware that I left sitting on the kitchen counter."

"Now, wait a minute," Gordon protested. "Let's not get the cart before the horse here. Piper has to open her presents first. Then I want to see twenty-seven candles on that cake and all of them lit."

"Talk about taking the joy out of your birthday!" Piper protested.

"It only gets worse from here on, kiddo," Gordon

advised. He waved Jeanette toward the kitchen, saying, "Just put that ice cream in the freezer for now."

"Oh, all right, spoilsport."

Gordon winked at a grinning Thai. "Just doing my duty as a pesky brother."

Piper rolled her eyes and let herself be herded into the living room along with her parents. Gordon put her in the armchair, the "seat of honor," as he termed it. Then the presents came out. As they piled the three small boxes, each accompanied by a card, in her lap, she made a halfhearted protest.

"You know you shouldn't spend your money like this."

"Then how should we be spending it?" Ransome wanted to know, dropping a kiss on the top of her head. She had worn her hair caught loosely at the nape of her neck with a barrette that he had specifically chosen as a Christmas gift for her, and she couldn't help thinking to herself that life was good again.

They had come a long way together. Asia would always be missed, but only his physical presence was lacking. In spirit, he would always be with them, and one day he would welcome each of them into paradise, where they would be together for eternity. In truth, the family was closer now than they ever had been, and each of them had grown markedly in faith, especially Thai, but no more surely than she.

Her spirit had found the conduit of prayer again. Once, talking to God had been much like conversing with an old friend. Now her communication with the Almighty had deepened. When she went to her knees these days, even figuratively, she truly felt as if she stood before the mercy seat of the Most High God, and more often than not she found herself simply praising rather than petitioning Him.

She had much to be thankful for, including the gifts stacked in her lap.

"This one first," Charlotte said, reaching for the bottom box. She pressed the small square box and its accompanying card into Piper's hands.

Piper read the card first. Tears stood in her eyes by the time she finished, but they were glad tears and quickly blinked away even before she turned her attention to the box itself. Carefully, her anticipation growing, she picked at the seam in the paper. A metallic green, it was almost too pretty to tear, but in the end her enthusiasm won out and she wound up ripping it anyway. She lifted the lid on the white box and found a golden bracelet nestled on cotton inside. Several charms had been attached to it—symbols of her faith and profession and one that was engraved with the shape of a sandpiper and the word "Thailand."

"Oh, it's lovely!"

Her father rose to help her put it on. "Mother and I thought you might like it."

She turned her face up for his kiss. "It's beautiful, Dad. Thank you." She fingered the round Thailand charm and sensed her mother's hand. "Did you design this, Mom?"

Charlotte nodded and came forward to hug her. "It seemed appropriate."

"It's beautiful. I love it. Thank you."

The next box was the smallest, another square, no more than an inch and a half across, if that. The sweet card attached was signed by her sister-in-law and brother. After reading the card, she slit the paper with a fingernail and peeled it back. Obviously the family had planned their gifts together, so she wasn't surprised when she found another charm. This one had Asia's picture inside a tiny frame. His smile seemed serene and pleased. The tears returned to her eyes.

"How special! What a wonderful gift. But now I must have charms with photos of all of you, too."

"Ta-da!" Thai said, snatching the last box and handing it back to her.

"Really? That's what this is?" she asked, eagerly shredding the paper. She opened the box to find six more charms, all identical except for the photos contained in each. One was empty—an extra, she supposed, in case she lost one of the others. "This is just perfect! Oh, I can't thank you all enough."

She opened her arms and her family engulfed her. Thai was on his knees in front of her, leaving her mother and sister-in-law to come at her from the sides and her father to bend over her chair from the back. Only Gordon hung back. After dispensing hugs to the others, she looked to him, puzzled at his seeming reluctance.

"Gordo?"

"Always jumping the gun," he admonished teasingly. "You're not through yet. You have another gift, a very special one." Oddly, he seemed to choke up then. After clearing his throat, he managed to add, "You could say this one is from Asia."

One hand rose to cover her heart, the other her mouth. Tears, still never far from the surface, gathered once more. "You'd better just tell me what it is first."

"It's not a what, my dear," said her father.

She looked to him and saw the same light in his

eyes as Gordon's. "Not a *what?*" she repeated carefully.

"A *who*," her mother said gently.

Piper studied her mother's face for a moment, seeing a softness and understanding there that made her pulse speed up.

"That," said a deep, much beloved voice, "would be me."

Piper twisted around in the chair. Mitch stood in the center of the wide, arched doorway, looking a little uncomfortable, a smile on his face.

"Mitch!"

She literally launched herself across the room, her feet hardly touching the floor at all. He opened his arms and caught her, rocking slightly as her weight hit him. Chuckling, he held her tightly.

"Happy birthday, sweetheart."

"Oh, Mitch! You're here! I can't believe you're here!"

"Where else would I be today of all days?" he asked softly. She laughed and wrapped her arms around his neck, so happy she could burst.

Had he really doubted his welcome? he asked himself as her family gathered around them, all talking at once.

"Do you know how hard it is to keep somebody that big under wraps?" Thai was asking no one in particular. He was a good-looking kid, clean-cut, with his mother's warm brown hair and eyes a little darker than Piper's.

"Just think if you'd had to put him in a box," Jeanette teased. A small, pretty brunette, she seemed to have a lively wit beneath that calm, unruffled exterior.

"That would be some bow!" Gordon quipped, his brassy hair a pleasing contrast to his wife's more muted medium brown.

"It's good to see you again, Mitch," Mr. Wynne said warmly, offering his hand. He was a tall, rawboned man whose build had nothing in common with that of either his daughter or son, both of whom possessed their mother's more solid frame. Of course, they had gotten their hair from him, though age had dimmed and thinned Ransome's thatch.

"The pleasure's all mine, sir."

Mitch shifted Piper to his side and clasped Mr. Wynne's hand, one arm still about her waist. He hoped Wynne didn't think he was forward, but he couldn't quite seem to let her go just yet—and she didn't seem inclined to be let go.

Mrs. Wynne offered her own hand, and Mitch had no choice then but to remove his arm from Piper's waist in order to take the hands of both her parents. The older woman was the mold from which Piper had been made. Her thick white hair had been cut short and left to wave about her head, framing the face that Piper herself would wear in a few decades. It was a face he thought he could gladly spend the rest of his life with.

"Mrs. Wynne. You're looking well, ma'am."

She seemed amused, as if she knew that he was seeing Piper in her. "I'll look a sight better after I've had some cake," she proclaimed.

"And ice cream!" Thai added enthusiastically.

"Candles first," Gordon insisted, adding playfully, "Somebody get the fire extinguisher."

Everyone bustled into the dining room, leaving him and Piper to bring up the rear.

"I can't believe you're here!" she said again, keeping her voice low. "When you didn't write or call, I thought—"

"We can talk about that later," he said, wrapping his arm around her waist again. He just couldn't help touching her. If he had his way, they'd be joined at the hip from now on. But it remained to be seen if he was going to have his way in this. He couldn't help worrying that he hadn't given her enough time, although it had been all he could do to stay away this long.

Jeanette was sticking candles into the top of the cake when they reached the dining room, but before he'd let her light them, Gordon insisted on counting them to be sure that she hadn't left one off. Piper just laughed. Then as Jeanette patiently lit one candle after the other, Piper looked to her brother and said with jovial promise, "Wait until March."

Mitch assumed that Gordon's birthday was the next month, an assumption that Thai confirmed by crowing, "Ho, Dad! We'd better have the fire department on standby before we light that baby up!"

Everyone laughed, but then the candles were all lit, and it was time for the obligatory wish. Piper folded her hands and closed her eyes. It was her birthday, but Mitch found himself making a "wish" of his own.

Forgive me if I'm being selfish, Lord. I have tried to be patient, and I've tried to believe that I can give her up if You have a purpose for her that doesn't include me. But, oh, how I want her!

Opening her eyes again, Piper drew a deep breath

and blew out all the candles. Mitch applauded along with everyone else.

"Now," Jeanette said, "if someone will just say a blessing over this cake, we'll get to cutting and eating."

To Mitch's surprise, the three elder Wynnes looked straight at him. Wondering if he were being put to the test somehow, he nodded, accepting the commission gladly.

Linking arms around the table, they all bowed their heads.

"Gracious Lord God," he began, feeling, as always, that he had moved into the very presence of holiness, "I thank You for this family and all that they have meant to Your kingdom. They've had some tough times, Lord, but they've clung to Your promises, and I know You honor and reward their faith. Go with Piper over this next year. Make this the best year yet for her and her loved ones and keep us all ever in the palm of Your hand. Amen."

"Amen," said the others. Then Ransome lifted a hand in a signal that he would speak.

"You know, God never promised us a life of ease and fun without hardship or grief of any sort, but He did promise always to be with us and to fulfill our every need. Sometimes in the midst of our pain it seems that He's falling down on the job, but just look at us now. He's used tragedy to bring us all closer to Him and to each other—and to bring Mitch into our lives. God always provides for the happiness of His children, even in the midst of sadness." He looked at Piper and said, "This is a happy day. I want you all to enjoy it."

"Thank you, Daddy," Piper said softly, leaning in to kiss his cheek.

"Now give me some cake," Ransome demanded gruffly, and everyone laughed again.

In due course the cake was cut and the ice cream was dished out. Thai ate two pieces of cake and about a half gallon of ice cream. Jeanette made a pot of coffee to warm them all after the cold treat, though the weather had turned mild and calm, mild enough that Mitch felt safe in suggesting that he and Piper drink their coffee outside.

"That sounds good," she said, rising and leading him from the room. She reached into the coat closet for a bulky knit cardigan to protect her from the chill, shrugging into it while he held her cup.

He made do with his suit coat, figuring that as long as they stayed in the sunshine, they would be quite comfortable.

It was a breathtakingly beautiful day, with sunlight like golden crystal and air as soft as down. Overhead the sky made a deep blue bowl with only a few white wisps of cloud to mar it.

"I still can't believe you came all this way for my birthday," she said as they strolled toward a bench-type glider in a sunny corner of the backyard.

"I wanted to come sooner," he said, "but I couldn't let myself get in the way."

"You could never be in the way, Mitch."

He thanked her with a look, but then he said, "Yes, I could. I worry even now that I haven't given you enough time to heal."

She sighed as she sank onto the wooden seat, her

coffee cup held carefully in front of her. "You of all people should know that it's a lifelong process."

"Yes, I do understand that," he said, taking the seat next to her, his own cup balanced in his left hand. "But there is a point when coping is the most important thing, and it's easy to get thrown off by other issues."

She nodded, sipped from her cup and said, "I wasn't coping very well when we met. I wasn't coping with Asia's death at all."

"You were doing the best you could on your own," he argued gently.

"But I wasn't on my own," she said, looking at him. "I had you from the very beginning."

He looked into his cup as if searching for the future there. "I don't believe that was an accident, Piper— the way we met, me finding that letter and feeling so convinced that I had to return it to its owner."

"No accident," she confirmed softly.

He leaned forward and set his coffee cup in the pale, brittle grass at his feet. Then he sat back again, lifting one arm to curve it around her shoulders.

"You can't know how much I've missed you," he said. "I didn't call or write because I knew that if I did I wouldn't be able to stay away as long as you needed me to."

"I wasn't sure what to think," she confessed, laying her head on his shoulder, "but I understand now."

"I've prayed about this daily, and I've been in touch with Gordon all along."

"Oh?" She was understandably surprised, but he was obviously trying to make a point.

"Your brother says you still don't know what to

do with yourself, where you belong, what God intends for your life.''

She lifted her head and looked at him. ''He's wrong. I know exactly where I belong.''

He looked for an instant as if she'd hit him. ''You do? H-have you told your family?''

She shook her head, uncertain what was bothering him.

''C-can you tell me?'' He didn't sound as if he really wanted to know.

She shifted slightly and reached right past him with the hand holding her coffee cup. She turned her wrist and poured the coffee on the ground before setting the cup on the flat armrest of the glider.

''I belong,'' she said huskily, ''wherever you are.''

He stared at her blankly for a moment, as if he hadn't understood, and then he sucked in a sharp, deep breath. ''Thank God! All this time I've been telling Him that I could give you up if that's what He wanted. A-are you sure that you're not called to the mission field or—?''

''Quite sure,'' she interrupted, struggling with a smile.

''I—I want to give you time to r-really get to know me, to figure out exactly how you feel. If I'm rushing you, honey, just say the word and I'll back off.''

''Mitch,'' she said patiently, ''do you know what I wished before I blew out the candles?''

He shook his head, grinning like an idiot. ''What?''

''I wished you'd get a clue and kiss me before I get any older.''

His jaw dropped, and then he closed his arms around her and pulled her to him, bending his head to hers.

More than their lips melded in that kiss. Their futures joined, inextricably woven together into a single pattern, what they thought their life together would be.

They would have love, that kiss said, and true joining in every sense of the word—the best of all this world had to offer and the next, as well. They would have common purpose and combined strength, enough to see them through the rough patches and make them fully appreciate the smooth ones. They would have love in all its guises, its fullest expression, its smallest duty, its eternal ramifications. They would have each other and the guidance of a mutually known Lord, in Whom they would be made complete, a single entity with two satisfied souls.

He poured out promise, and she soaked it all up, right into the very core of her being.

"I love you," he said, finally breaking the kiss.

"I love you, too."

"I know." He pressed his forehead to hers. "I mean, I thought I knew. All this time I've been hoping that you meant that the way I wanted you to mean it."

She drew back a little. "You heard me?"

"Absolutely, I heard you. Didn't you mean for me to?"

"No. I mean, yes, but I didn't think you would."

"How do you think I'd have gotten through these months without you if I hadn't had that to hang on to?" he asked. "To find you just when I felt God finally telling me that He had more in store for me than work and dealing with other people's grief and then to let you go again! I had to use every scrap of faith I could pull together. I can't tell you how many times I had to get down on my knees and beg God for the patience to get through this."

And to think that she had felt abandoned!

But no, not really. Deep down in her heart of hearts she had always known that they would be together. In some ways she had known even before he had dropped into that seat beside her, a slip of paper with healing on it tucked into his pocket. She had tried to forget for a while, tried to believe that God was not in control of a world where bad things could happen to good people and pain must come at some point to all. Even then, in the secret places that she feared even to acknowledge, she had known she wasn't alone, would never be alone. God did not abandon His own or fail to provide for their every need.

She had come through the valley the same way that Mitch had, on faith, and as God would have it, they'd both come out at the same place.

"Oh, Mitch," she exclaimed, "I'm so thankful you were on that plane with me that day!"

"Sweetheart," he said, grinning, "I'm just glad it's still flying in both directions. I feel some frequent flyer miles coming on."

She laughed, too happy to hold it in anymore, quite sure, finally, in a joy that even sorrow could not diminish so long as faith and love were given free rein.

Epilogue

$\sim$

Mₐy was the perfect month for a wedding in Texas, and the candlelit church was packed, even if it was pouring rain outside. The wedding coordinator, who was keeping time with the music, stood poised in front of a pair of exquisitely carved double doors. At precisely the right moment she pulled them wide and stepped back. On her father's arm, Piper moved into position. Pausing a moment, she took in the scene into which she was about to step.

Every pew was filled. Banks of candles flickered, spreading romantic light throughout the hall. Mitch stood at the head of the aisle, handsome in a sedate black double-breasted tuxedo and white bow tie, looking as relaxed as if he were in his own living room. He was flanked on one side by Thai, his cousin Jack, a spiffed-up Scott Ninever and a good friend from church, on the other by Melissa, Jeanette and two longtime friends of Piper's dressed identically in evening gowns of spring green. Directly behind him stood Gordon in formal robes, a Bible in his hands.

Their eyes met and held across the crowded sanctuary bedecked with yellow roses as the string quartet paused in their playing. Piper smiled and felt the encouraging pat of her father's hand on her arm. Then a lone violin began a slow, dreamy rendition of the wedding march. Piper lifted her left hand and turned her wrist. Asia's tiny face smiled at her from the charm dangling from her bracelet. She shared her answering smile with her father, and together they stepped off. At the same moment Gordon signaled the crowd, and the throng of witnesses rose to their feet in a hushed, rippling wave of excitement.

She took her time, savoring every moment of that long walk to the altar. Along the way she smiled and nodded at good friends, old and new, many of whom had made the trip from Dallas for the wedding, including Ivan Sontag and his great-grandson Robin, who would have darted out into the aisle to hug her and crush her belled white chiffon skirts if Red hadn't laid a patient, restraining hand on his shoulder. She gave him a bright smile, making a mental note to find him later at the reception.

Then her gaze fell on her mother's face. From the foremost pew, Charlotte smiled, her innate strength and calm faith radiating outward. Across the aisle from her, Vernon Sayer literally beamed while Marian dabbed at her happy tears with a lace-edged handkerchief. By prearrangement, Piper paused and tugged two orange-gold roses from her otherwise white bridal bouquet. Being careful of the long chiffon veil streaming down her back, she gave each with a kiss to the moms, the first to her own mother, the second to Mitch's. Then two more steps brought her to her future.

Mitch moved forward, his gaze meeting hers, his smile serene. Gordon lifted his voice.

"Who gives this woman in marriage?"

"Her mother and I." Ransome placed her hand in Mitch's and backed away.

Gordon seated the audience and beckoned the beaming couple forward. Not quite forty minutes later he pronounced them husband and wife. Mitch smiled down at her, gathered her into his arms and kissed her until everyone started to laugh, including the two of them.

Gordon made the formal announcement. "Ladies and gentlemen, I give you Mr. and Mrs. Mitchell Sayer."

The applause and the music swelled simultaneously. Still laughing, Piper snagged her bouquet from a teary-eyed Melissa as she and Mitch rushed down the aisle, hand in hand. They hit the foyer at a near run. He swung her back into his arms, kissed her hard, hugged her tight.

"You are stunning today! Stunning! I've never seen a more beautiful bride!"

"I'm so glad you think so."

"I know so."

"Thank you. Husband."

He cupped her face in his hands, bending close just as Melissa and Thai burst through the swinging doors. Taking his role as honorary best man very seriously, Thai immediately began shooing them toward a small room where they could wait, out of sight, while the remaining bridal party and their parents reversed the processional and the guests dispersed. Before joining their friends and extended families for dinner and cel-

ebration at the reception, they would pose for a few—
a very few, at Mitch's insistence—formal photos.

They closed the door behind them, instructing Thai
to let them know the moment that the sanctuary was
empty and the photographer and wedding coordinator
were ready for them. In the meantime, they had a few
precious moments to themselves.

"I'm married!" Mitch exclaimed, wrapping his
arms around her.

"That makes two of us," she teased.

He laughed and kissed her again before checking
his watch. "Remember, we're out of the reception by
nine o'clock."

She saluted smartly, barely controlling her smile.
"Aye, aye, husband sir."

"My wife," he said dreamily, squeezing her hands.

Thai tapped on the door. "You two ready?"

"Almost," Mitch called, reaching for the shoes
he'd stashed under a chair in the corner. "Make sure
everyone's in place, Thai, and that the limo's waiting
under the canopy."

"Sure thing."

Mitch stepped out of the shoes he was wearing and
into the others, which were very nearly identical, as
Piper quickly sat and traded her soft cloth slippers for
white leather. He pulled her up and helped straighten
her skirts, then gave her a wink. She laughed, remembering the tube she'd given him to hold for her the
day before.

"I'd better check my lipstick."

He plucked it from his coat pocket, his gold-and-
silver wedding band glinting in the overhead light.

She admired the reflection of her own matching
band and the extravagant engagement ring as she

quickly repaired her lipstick. Was that happy, sophisticated-looking woman really her? With her shoulders bared and most of her hair coiled atop her head inside a crown of pearls that anchored the flowing chiffon veil, she looked like a princess in a fairy tale.

"Ready?" he asked, taking her hand in his.

"Ready."

They hurried back to the sanctuary to pose. The photographer would have dawdled over every photo, but Mitch wouldn't allow it. He was a man with a purpose. Piper didn't mind in the least. She couldn't wait to be alone with him, either.

"That's it," the photographer finally announced.

Piper shared a conspiratorial smile with her husband and said, "One more."

"Stay where you are," Mitch instructed the puzzled photographer.

Piper gave him her hand, and he led her to the altar. A wink and a smile, then Piper lifted her skirts and they knelt together.

"Mitchell Sayer!" Marian scolded, her voice rich with laughter.

"And no retouch," he insisted around a grin.

Piper bowed her head, but her shoulders were shaking.

The photographer snapped the picture.

It would always be their favorite wedding photo—the two of them kneeling at the altar of their Lord, hands clasped. Printed on the soles of their shoes in their own hands were the clearly readable words "Love is no accident."

For two children of God, no truer words had ever been written.

* * * * *

Dear Reader,

The Twenty-Third Psalm is a familiar passage of Scripture beloved by generations. Like many, I memorized that eloquent Old Testament chapter as a child but had difficulty relating to it. I couldn't conceive of death, let alone the "valley of the shadow of death," and I had no enemies. Even taken allegorically, neither term seemed applicable to anyone I knew. Thankfully, I reached adulthood before I came to a personal understanding of the concepts involved. When I got to that point, this Psalm (along with other precious Scriptures) helped me remember the sufficiency and intention of God's love for us.

Some find the concept of a loving God who can and will allow tragedy into our lives for reasons that we cannot always comprehend to be an impossible contradiction, and yet every successful parent knows what strength, wisdom and love are required to allow a child to learn by suffering. Of course, we do everything in our power to minimize our children's pain, but some very necessary lessons, like learning how to deal with loss, can only be accomplished via experience.

Thankfully God loves us enough, as Mitch and Piper's story demonstrates, to supply our *every* need, and that includes joy. He wants the very best for us, and, remember, sweet is best when it follows sour. I hope I've given you a taste of each and that you always have more of the sweet!

God Bless,

Arlene James

FIRST MATES

BY

CECELIA
DOWDY

Cruising the Caribbean was just what Rainy Jackson needed
to get over her faithless ex-fiancé…and meeting handsome
fellow passenger Winston Michaels didn't hurt, either! As a
new Christian, Winston was looking to reflect on his own
losses. Yet as the two spent some time together both on the
ship and back home in Miami, he soon realized he wanted
Rainy along to share his life voyage.

Don't miss FIRST MATES
On sale February 2005

Available at your favorite retail outlet.

Take 2 inspirational love stories FREE!

PLUS get a FREE surprise gift!

Mail to Steeple Hill Reader Service™

In U.S.
3010 Walden Ave.
P.O. Box 1867
Buffalo, NY 14240-1867

In Canada
P.O. Box 609
Fort Erie, Ontario
L2A 5X3

YES! Please send me 2 free Love Inspired® novels and my free surprise gift. After receiving them, if I don't wish to receive anymore, I can return the shipping statement marked cancel. If I don't cancel, I will receive 4 brand-new novels every month, before they're available in stores! Bill me at the low price of $4.24 each in the U.S. and $4.74 each in Canada, plus 25¢ shipping and handling and applicable sales tax, if any*. That's the complete price and a savings of over 10% off the cover prices—quite a bargain! I understand that accepting the books and gift places me under no obligation ever to buy any books. I can always return a shipment and cancel at any time. Even if I never buy another book from Steeple Hill, the 2 free books and the surprise gift are mine to keep forever.

113 IDN DZ9M
313 IDN DZ9N

Name	(PLEASE PRINT)	
Address	Apt. No.	
City	State/Prov.	Zip/Postal Code

Not valid to current Love Inspired® subscribers.

Want to try two free books from another series?
Call 1-800-873-8635 or visit www.morefreebooks.com.

* Terms and prices are subject to change without notice. Sales tax applicable in New York. Canadian residents will be charged applicable provincial taxes and GST. All orders subject to approval. Offer limited to one per household.

® are registered trademarks owned and used by the trademark owner and or its licensee.

INTLI04R

©2004 Steeple Hill

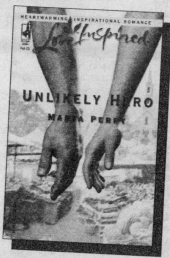